# FIRST LOVE

INCLUDING THE ILLUSTRATED ESSAY 'A NOTE ON LITERATURE'

D1733339

*by*

## IVAN TURGENEV

**COMPASS CIRCLE**

**First Love.**
Written by Ivan Turgenev.
Translated by Isabel Hapgood.
Current edition published by Compass Circle in 2022.

Published by Compass Circle
Cover copyright ©2022 by Compass Circle.

Note:
All efforts have been made to preserve original spellings and punctuation of the original edition which may include old-fashioned English spellings of words and archaic variants.

This book is a product of its time and does not reflect the same views on race, gender, sexuality, ethnicity, and interpersonal relations as it would if it were written today.

For information contact :
information@compass-circle.com

*There is a sweetness in being the sole source, the autocratic and irresponsible cause of the greatest joy and profoundest pain to another.*

IVAN TURGENEV

# SECRET WISDOM OF THE AGES SERIES

Life presents itself, it advances in a fast way. Life indeed never stops. It never stops until the end. The most diverse questions peek and fade in our minds. Sometimes we seek for answers. Sometimes we just let time go by.

The book you have now in your hands has been waiting to be discovered by you. This book may reveal the answers to some of your questions.

Books are friends. Friends who are always by your side and who can give you great ideas, advice or just comfort your soul.

A great book can make you see things in your soul that you have not yet discovered, make you see things in your soul that you were not aware of.

Great books can change your life for the better. They can make you understand fascinating theories, give you new ideas, inspire you to undertake new challenges or to walk along new paths.

Literature Classics like the one of *First Love* are indeed a secret to many, but for those of us lucky enough to have discovered them, by one way or another, these books can enlighten us. They can open a wide range of possibilities to us. Because achieving greatness requires knowledge.

The series SECRET WISDOM OF THE AGES presented by Compass Circle try to bring you the great timeless masterpieces of literature, autobiographies and personal development,.

We welcome you to discover with us fascinating works by Nathaniel Hawthorne, Sir Arthur Conan Doyle, Edith Wharton, among others.

# Contents

# IVAN TURGENEV

Born   Ivan Sergeyevich Turgenev
November 9, 1818
Oryol, Russia

Died   September 3, 1883
Bougival, France

IVAN TURGENEV

# FIRST LOVE

THE guests had long since departed. The clock struck half-past twelve. There remained in the room only the host, Sergyéi Nikoláevitch, and Vladímir Petróvitch.

The host rang and ordered the remains of the supper to be removed.—"So then, the matter is settled,"—he said, ensconcing himself more deeply in his arm-chair, and lighting a cigar:—"each of us is to narrate the history of his first love. 'Tis your turn, Sergyéi Nikoláevitch."

Sergyéi Nikoláevitch, a rather corpulent man, with a plump, fair-skinned face, first looked at the host, then raised his eyes to the ceiling.—"I had no first love,"—he began at last:—"I began straight off with the second."

"How was that?"

"Very simply. I was eighteen years of age when, for the first time, I dangled after a very charming young lady; but I courted her as though it were no new thing to me: exactly as I courted others afterward. To tell the truth, I fell in love, for the first and last time, at the age of six, with my nurse;—but that is a very long time ago. The details of our relations have been erased from my memory; but even if I remembered them, who would be interested in them?"

"Then what are we to do?"—began the host.—"There was nothing very startling about my first love either; I never fell in love with any one before Anna Ivánovna, now my wife; and everything ran as though on oil with us; our fathers made up the match, we very promptly fell in love with

3

each other, and entered the bonds of matrimony without delay. My story can be told in two words. I must confess, gentlemen, that in raising the question of first love, I set my hopes on you, I will not say old, but yet no longer young bachelors. Will not you divert us with something, Vladímir Petróvitch?"

"My first love belongs, as a matter of fact, not altogether to the ordinary category,"—replied, with a slight hesitation, Vladímir Petróvitch, a man of forty, whose black hair was sprinkled with grey.

"Ah!"—said the host and Sergyéi Nikoláevitch in one breath.—"So much the better.... Tell us."

"As you like ... or no: I will not narrate; I am no great hand at telling a story; it turns out dry and short, or long-drawn-out and artificial. But if you will permit me, I will write down all that I remember in a note-book, and will read it aloud to you."

At first the friends would not consent, but Vladímir Petróvitch insisted on having his own way. A fortnight later they came together again, and Vladímir Sergyéitch kept his promise.

This is what his note-book contained.

# I

I was sixteen years old at the time. The affair took place in the summer of 1833.

I was living in Moscow, in my parents' house. They had hired a villa near the Kalúga barrier, opposite the Neskútchny Park.[1]—I was preparing for the university, but

---

[1] The finest of the public parks in Moscow, situated near the famous

was working very little and was not in a hurry.

No one restricted my freedom. I had done whatever I pleased ever since I had parted with my last French governor, who was utterly unable to reconcile himself to the thought that he had fallen "like a bomb" (*comme une bombe*) into Russia, and with a stubborn expression on his face, wallowed in bed for whole days at a time. My father treated me in an indifferently-affectionate way; my mother paid hardly any attention to me, although she had no children except me: other cares engrossed her. My father, still a young man and very handsome, had married her from calculation; she was ten years older than he. My mother led a melancholy life: she was incessantly in a state of agitation, jealousy, and wrath—but not in the presence of my father; she was very much afraid of him, and he maintained a stern, cold, and distant manner.... I have never seen a man more exquisitely calm, self-confident, and self-controlled.

I shall never forget the first weeks I spent at the villa. The weather was magnificent; we had left town the ninth of May, on St. Nicholas's day. I rambled,—sometimes in the garden of our villa, sometimes in Neskútchny Park, sometimes beyond the city barriers; I took with me some book or other,—a course of Kaidánoff,—but rarely opened it, and chiefly recited aloud poems, of which I knew a great many by heart. The blood was fermenting in me, and my heart was aching—so sweetly and absurdly; I was always waiting for something, shrinking at something, and wondering at everything, and was all ready for anything at a moment's

Sparrow Hills, is called "Neskútchny"—"Not Tiresome," generally rendered "Sans Souci." It contains an imperial residence, the Alexander Palace, used as an official summer home by the Governor-General of Moscow.—Translator.

notice. My fancy was beginning to play, and hovered swiftly ever around the selfsame image, as martins hover round a belfry at sunset. But even athwart my tears and athwart the melancholy, inspired now by a melodious verse, now by the beauty of the evening, there peered forth, like grass in springtime, the joyous sensation of young, bubbling life.

I had a saddle-horse; I was in the habit of saddling it myself, and when I rode off alone as far as possible, in some direction, launching out at a gallop and fancying myself a knight at a tourney—how blithely the wind whistled in my ears!—Or, turning my face skyward, I welcomed its beaming light and azure into my open soul.

I remember, at that time, the image of woman, the phantom of woman's love, almost never entered my mind in clearly-defined outlines; but in everything I thought, in everything I felt, there lay hidden the half-conscious, shame-faced presentiment of something new, inexpressibly sweet, feminine....

This presentiment, this expectation permeated my whole being; I breathed it, it coursed through my veins in every drop of blood ... it was fated to be speedily realised.

Our villa consisted of a wooden manor-house with columns, and two tiny outlying wings; in the wing to the left a tiny factory of cheap wall-papers was installed.... More than once I went thither to watch how half a score of gaunt, dishevelled young fellows in dirty smocks and with tipsy faces were incessantly galloping about at the wooden levers which jammed down the square blocks of the press, and in that manner, by the weight of their puny bodies, printed the motley-hued patterns of the wall-papers. The wing on the right stood empty and was for rent. One day—three weeks after the ninth of May—the shutters on the windows of this wing were opened, and women's faces made their appearance in them; some family or other had moved into it. I remember how, that same day at dinner, my mother inquired of the butler who our new neighbours were, and on hearing the name of Princess Zasyékin, said at first, not without some respect:—"Ah! a Princess" ... and then she added:—"She must be some poor person!"

"They came in three hired carriages, ma'am,"—remarked the butler, as he respectfully presented a dish. "They have no carriage of their own, ma'am, and their furniture is of the very plainest sort."

"Yes,"—returned my mother,—"and nevertheless, it is better so."

My father shot a cold glance at her; she subsided into silence.

As a matter of fact, Princess Zasyékin could not be a wealthy woman: the wing she had hired was so old and tiny and low-roofed that people in the least well-to-do would not have been willing to inhabit it.—However, I let this go in at one ear and out at the other. The princely title had little effect on me: I had recently been reading Schiller's "The Brigands."

## II

I had a habit of prowling about our garden every evening, gun in hand, and standing guard against the crows.—I had long cherished a hatred for those wary, rapacious and crafty birds. On the day of which I have been speaking, I went into the garden as usual, and, after having fruitlessly made the round of all the alleys (the crows recognised me from afar, and merely cawed spasmodically at a distance), I accidentally approached the low fence which separated *our* territory from the narrow strip of garden extending behind the right-hand wing and appertaining to it. I was walking along with drooping head. Suddenly I heard voices: I glanced over the fence—and was petrified.... A strange spectacle presented itself to me.

A few paces distant from me, on a grass-plot between green raspberry-bushes, stood a tall, graceful young girl, in a striped, pink frock and with a white kerchief on her head; around her pressed four young men, and she was tapping them in turn on the brow with those small grey flowers, the name of which I do not know, but which are familiar to children; these little flowers form tiny sacs, and burst with a pop when they are struck against anything hard. The young men offered their foreheads to her so willingly, and in the girl's movements (I saw her form in profile) there was something so bewitching, caressing, mocking, and charming, that I almost cried aloud in wonder and pleasure; and I believe I would have given everything in the world if those lovely little fingers had only consented to tap me on the brow. My gun slid down on the grass, I forgot everything, I devoured with my eyes that slender waist, and the neck and the beautiful arms, and the slightly ruffled fair hair, the intelligent eyes and those lashes, and the delicate cheek beneath them....

"Young man, hey there, young man!"—suddenly spoke up a voice near me:—"Is it permissible to stare like that at strange young ladies?"

I trembled all over, I was stupefied.... Beside me, on the other side of the fence, stood a man with closely-clipped black hair, gazing ironically at me. At that same moment, the young girl turned toward me.... I beheld huge grey eyes in a mobile, animated face—and this whole face suddenly began to quiver, and to laugh, and the white teeth gleamed from it, the brows elevated themselves in an amusing way.... I flushed, picked up my gun from the ground, and, pursued by ringing but not malicious laughter, I ran to my own room, flung myself on the bed, and covered my face with my hands. My heart was fairly leaping within me; I felt very much ashamed and very merry: I experienced an unprecedented emotion.

After I had rested awhile, I brushed my hair, made myself neat and went down-stairs to tea. The image of the young girl floated in front of me; my heart had ceased to leap, but ached in an agreeable sort of way.

"What ails thee?"—my father suddenly asked me:—"hast thou killed a crow?"

I was on the point of telling him all, but refrained and only smiled to myself. As I was preparing for bed, I whirled round thrice on one foot, I know not why, pomaded my hair, got into bed and slept all night like a dead man. Toward morning I awoke for a moment, raised my head, cast a glance of rapture around me—and fell asleep again.

### III

"How am I to get acquainted with them?" was my first thought, as soon as I awoke in the morning. I went out into the garden before tea, but did not approach too close to the fence, and saw no one. After tea I walked several times up and down the street in front of the villa, and cast a distant glance at the windows.... I thought I descried *her* face behind the curtains, and retreated with all possible despatch. "But I must get acquainted,"—I thought, as I walked with irregular strides up and down the sandy stretch which extends in front of the Neskútchny Park ... "but how? that is the question." I recalled the most trifling incidents of the meeting on the previous evening; for some reason, her manner of laughing at me presented itself to me with particular clearness.... But while I was fretting thus and constructing various plans, Fate was already providing for me.

During my absence, my mother had received a letter from her new neighbour on grey paper sealed with brown wax, such as is used only on postal notices, and on the corks of cheap wine. In this letter, written in illiterate language, and with a slovenly chirography, the Princess requested my mother to grant her her protection: my mother, according to the Princess's words, was well acquainted with the prominent people on whom the fortune of herself and her children depended, as she had some extremely important law-suits: "I apeal tyou,"—she wrote,—"as a knoble woman to a knoble woman, and moarover, it is agriable to me to makeus of this oportunity." In conclusion, she asked permission of my mother to call upon her. I found my mother in an unpleasant frame of mind: my father was not at home, and she had no one with whom to take counsel. It was impossible not to reply to a "knoble woman," and to a Princess into the bargain; but how to reply perplexed my mother.

It seemed to her ill-judged to write a note in French, and my mother was not strong in Russian orthography herself—and was aware of the fact—and did not wish to compromise herself. She was delighted at my arrival, and immediately ordered me to go to the Princess and explain to her verbally that my mother was always ready, to the extent of her ability, to be of service to Her Radiance,[2] and begged that she would call upon her about one o'clock.

This unexpectedly swift fulfilment of my secret wishes both delighted and frightened me; but I did not betray the emotion which held possession of me, and preliminarily betook myself to my room for the purpose of donning a new neckcloth and coat; at home I went about in a round-jacket and turn-over collars, although I detested them greatly.

## IV

In the cramped and dirty anteroom of the wing, which I entered with an involuntary trembling of my whole body, I was received by a grey-haired old serving-man with a face the hue of dark copper, pig-like, surly little eyes, and such deep wrinkles on his forehead as I had never seen before in my life. He was carrying on a platter the gnawed spinal bone of a herring, and, pushing to with his foot the door which led into the adjoining room, he said abruptly:—"What do you want?"

"Is Princess Zasyékin at home?"—I inquired.

"Vonifáty!"—screamed a quavering female voice on the other side of the door.

---

[2]Princes, princesses, counts, and countesses have the title of Siyátelstvo (siyám—to shine, to be radiant); generally translated "Illustrious Highness" or "Serenity."—Translator.

The servant silently turned his back on me, thereby displaying the badly-worn rear of his livery with its solitary, rusted, armouried button, and went away, leaving the platter on the floor.

"Hast thou been to the police-station?"—went on that same feminine voice. The servant muttered something in reply.—"Hey?... Some one has come?"—was the next thing audible.... "The young gentleman from next door?—Well, ask him in."

"Please come into the drawing-room, sir,"—said the servant, making his appearance again before me, and picking up the platter from the floor. I adjusted my attire and entered the "drawing-room."

I found myself in a tiny and not altogether clean room, with shabby furniture which seemed to have been hastily set in place. At the window, in an easy-chair with a broken arm, sat a woman of fifty, with uncovered hair[3] and plain-featured, clad in an old green gown, and with a variegated worsted kerchief round her neck. Her small black eyes fairly bored into me.

I went up to her and made my bow.

"I have the honour of speaking to Princess Zasyékin?"

"I am Princess Zasyékin: and you are the son of Mr. B—?"

"Yes, madam. I have come to you with a message from my mother."

"Pray be seated. Vonifáty! where are my keys? Hast thou seen them?"

---

[3]The custom still prevails in Russia, to a great extent, for all elderly women to wear caps. In the peasant class it is considered as extremely indecorous to go "simple-haired," as the expression runs—Translator.

I communicated to Madame Zasyékin my mother's answer to her note. She listened to me, tapping the window-pane with her thick, red fingers, and when I had finished she riveted her eyes on me once more.

"Very good; I shall certainly go,"—said she at last.—"But how young you are still! How old are you, allow me to ask?"

"Sixteen,"—I replied with involuntary hesitation.

The Princess pulled out of her pocket some dirty, written documents, raised them up to her very nose and began to sort them over.

"'Tis a good age,"—she suddenly articulated, turning and fidgeting in her chair.—"And please do not stand on ceremony. We are plain folks."

"Too plain,"—I thought, with involuntary disgust taking in with a glance the whole of her homely figure.

At that moment, the other door of the drawing-room was swiftly thrown wide open, and on the threshold appeared the young girl whom I had seen in the garden the evening before. She raised her hand and a smile flitted across her face.

"And here is my daughter,"—said the Princess, pointing at her with her elbow.—"Zínotchka, the son of our neighbour, Mr. B—. What is your name, permit me to inquire?"

"Vladímir,"—I replied, rising and lisping with agitation.

"And your patronymic?"

"Petróvitch."

"Yes! I once had an acquaintance, a chief of police, whose name was Vladímir Petróvitch also. Vonifáty! don't hunt for the keys; the keys are in my pocket."

The young girl continued to gaze at me with the same

smile as before, slightly puckering up her eyes and bending her head a little on one side.

"I have already seen M'sieu Voldemar,"—she began. (The silvery tone of her voice coursed through me like a sweet chill.)—"Will you permit me to call you so?"

"Pray do, madam,"—I lisped.

"Where was that?"—asked the Princess.

The young Princess did not answer her mother.

"Are you busy now?"—she said, without taking her eyes off me.

"Not in the least, madam."

"Then will you help me to wind some wool?  Come hither, to me."

She nodded her head at me and left the drawing-room. I followed her.

In the room which we entered the furniture was a little better and was arranged with great taste.—But at that moment I was almost unable to notice anything; I moved as though in a dream and felt a sort of intense sensation of well-being verging on stupidity throughout my frame.

The young Princess sat down, produced a knot of red wool, and pointing me to a chair opposite her, she carefully unbound the skein and placed it on my hands. She did all this in silence, with a sort of diverting deliberation, and with the same brilliant and crafty smile on her slightly parted lips. She began to wind the wool upon a card doubled together, and suddenly illumined me with such a clear, swift glance, that I involuntarily dropped my eyes. When her eyes, which were generally half closed, opened to their full extent her face underwent a complete change; it was as though light had inundated it.

"What did you think of me yesterday, M'sieu Voldemar?"—she asked, after a brief pause.—"You certainly must have condemned me?"

"I ... Princess ... I thought nothing ... how can I...." I replied, in confusion.

"Listen,"—she returned.—"You do not know me yet; I want people always to speak the truth to me. You are sixteen, I heard, and I am twenty-one; you see that I am a great deal older than you, and therefore you must always speak the truth to me ... and obey me,"—she added.—"Look at me; why don't you look at me?"

I became still more confused; but I raised my eyes to hers, nevertheless. She smiled, only not in her former manner, but with a different, an approving smile.—"Look at me,"—she said, caressingly lowering her voice:—"I don't like that.... Your face pleases me; I foresee that we shall be friends. And do you like me?"—she added slyly.

"Princess...." I was beginning....

"In the first place, call me Zinaída Alexándrovna; and in the second place,—what sort of a habit is it for children"—(she corrected herself)—"for young men—not to say straight out what they feel? You do like me, don't you?"

Although it was very pleasant to me to have her talk so frankly to me, still I was somewhat nettled. I wanted to show her that she was not dealing with a small boy, and, assuming as easy and serious a mien as I could, I said:—"Of course I like you very much, Zinaída Alexándrovna; I have no desire to conceal the fact."

She shook her head, pausing at intervals.—"Have you a

governor?"—she suddenly inquired.

"No, I have not had a governor this long time past."

I lied: a month had not yet elapsed since I had parted with my Frenchman.

"Oh, yes, I see: you are quite grown up."

She slapped me lightly on the fingers.—"Hold your hands straight!"—And she busied herself diligently with winding her ball.

I took advantage of the fact that she did not raise her eyes, and set to scrutinising her, first by stealth, then more and more boldly. Her face seemed to me even more charming than on the day before: everything about it was so delicate, intelligent and lovely. She was sitting with her back to the window, which was hung with a white shade; a ray of sunlight making its way through that shade inundated with a flood of light her fluffy golden hair, her innocent neck, sloping shoulders, and calm, tender bosom.—I gazed at her—and how near and dear she became to me! It seemed to me both that I had known her for a long time and that I had known nothing and had not lived before she came.... She wore a rather dark, already shabby gown, with an apron; I believe I would willingly have caressed every fold of that gown and of that apron. The tips of her shoes peeped out from under her gown; I would have bowed down to those little boots.... "And here I sit, in front of her,"—I thought.—"I have become acquainted with her ... what happiness, my God!" I came near bouncing out of my chair with rapture, but I merely dangled my feet to and fro a little, like a child who is enjoying dainties.

I felt as much at my ease as a fish does in water, and I

would have liked never to leave that room again as long as I lived.

Her eyelids slowly rose, and again her brilliant eyes beamed caressingly before me, and again she laughed.

"How you stare at me!"—she said slowly, shaking her finger at me.

I flushed scarlet.... "She understands all, she sees all,"—flashed through my head. "And how could she fail to see and understand all?"

Suddenly there was a clattering in the next room, and a sword clanked.

"Zína!"—screamed the old Princess from the drawing-room.—"Byelovzóroff has brought thee a kitten."

"A kitten!"—cried Zinaída, and springing headlong from her chair, she flung the ball on my knees and ran out.

I also rose, and, laying the skein of wool on the window-sill, went into the drawing-room, and stopped short in amazement. In the centre of the room lay a kitten with outstretched paws; Zinaída was kneeling in front of it, and carefully raising its snout. By the side of the young Princess, taking up nearly the entire wall-space between the windows, was visible a fair-complexioned, curly-haired young man, a hussar, with a rosy face and protruding eyes.

"How ridiculous!"—Zinaída kept repeating:—"and its eyes are not grey, but green, and what big ears it has! Thank you, Viktór Egóritch! you are very kind."

The hussar, in whom I recognised one of the young men whom I had seen on the preceding evening, smiled and bowed, clicking his spurs and clanking the links of his sword as he did so.

"You were pleased to say yesterday that you wished to possess a striped kitten with large ears ... so I have got it, madam. Your word is my law."—And again he bowed.

The kitten mewed faintly, and began to sniff at the floor.

"He is hungry!"—cried Zinaída.—"Vonifáty! Sónya! bring some milk."

The chambermaid, in an old yellow gown and with a faded kerchief on her head, entered with a saucer of milk in her hand, and placed it in front of the kitten. The kitten quivered, blinked, and began to lap.

"What a rosy tongue it has,"—remarked Zinaída, bending her head down almost to the floor, and looking sideways at it, under its very nose.

The kitten drank its fill, and began to purr, affectedly contracting and relaxing its paws. Zinaída rose to her feet, and turning to the maid, said indifferently:—"Take it away."

"Your hand—in return for the kitten,"—said the hussar, displaying his teeth, and bending over the whole of his huge body, tightly confined in a new uniform.

"Both hands,"—replied Zinaída, offering him her hands. While he was kissing them, she gazed at me over his shoulder.

I stood motionless on one spot, and did not know whether to laugh or to say something, or to hold my peace. Suddenly, through the open door of the anteroom, the figure of our footman, Feódor, caught my eye. He was making signs to me. I mechanically went out to him.

"What dost thou want?"—I asked.

"Your mamma has sent for you,"—he said in a whisper.—"She is angry because you do not return with an answer."

"Why, have I been here long?"

"More than an hour."

"More than an hour!"—I repeated involuntarily, and returning to the drawing-room, I began to bow and scrape my foot.

"Where are you going?"—the young Princess asked me, with a glance at the hussar.

"I must go home, madam. So I am to say,"—I added, addressing the old woman,—"that you will call upon us at two o'clock."

"Say that, my dear fellow."

The old Princess hurriedly drew out her snuffbox, and took a pinch so noisily that I fairly jumped.—"Say that,"— she repeated, tearfully blinking and grunting.

I bowed once more, turned and left the room with the same sensation of awkwardness in my back which a very young man experiences when he knows that people are staring after him.

"Look here, M'sieu Voldemar, you must drop in to see us,"—called Zinaída, and again burst out laughing.

"What makes her laugh all the time?" I thought, as I wended my way home accompanied by Feódor, who said nothing to me, but moved along disapprovingly behind me. My mother reproved me, and inquired, with surprise, "What could I have been doing so long at the Princess's?" I made her no answer, and went off to my own room. I had suddenly grown very melancholy.... I tried not to weep.... I was jealous of the hussar.

## V

The Princess, according to her promise, called on my mother, and did not please her. I was not present at their meeting, but at table my mother narrated to my father that that Princess Zasyékin seemed to her a *femme très vulgaire*; that she had bored her immensely with her requests that she would intervene on her behalf with Prince Sergyéi; that she was always having such law-suits and affairs,—*de vilaines affaires d'argent*,—and that she must be a great rogue. But my mother added that she had invited her with her daughter to dine on the following day (on hearing the words "with her daughter," I dropped my nose into my plate),—because, notwithstanding, she was a neighbour, and with a name. Thereupon my father informed my mother that he now recalled who the lady was: that in his youth he had known the late Prince Zasyékin, a capitally-educated but flighty and captious man; that in society he was called *"le Parisien,"* because of his long residence in Paris; that he had been very wealthy, but had gambled away all his property—and, no one knew why, though probably it had been for the sake of the money,—"although he might have made a better choice,"—added my father, with a cold smile,—he had married the daughter of some clerk in a chancellery, and after his marriage had gone into speculation, and ruined himself definitively.

"'Tis a wonder she did not try to borrow money,"—remarked my mother.

"She is very likely to do it,"—said my father, calmly.—"Does she speak French?"

"Very badly."

"M-m-m. However, that makes no difference. I think thou saidst that thou hadst invited her daughter; some one assured me that she is a very charming and well-educated girl."

"Ah! Then she does not take after her mother."

"Nor after her father,"—returned my father.—"He was also well educated, but stupid."

My mother sighed, and became thoughtful. My father relapsed into silence. I felt very awkward during the course of that conversation.

After dinner I betook myself to the garden, but without my gun. I had pledged my word to myself that I would not go near the "Zasyékin garden"; but an irresistible force drew me thither, and not in vain. I had no sooner approached the fence than I caught sight of Zinaída. This time she was alone. She was holding a small book in her hands and strolling slowly along the path. She did not notice me. I came near letting her slip past; but suddenly caught myself up and coughed.

She turned round but did not pause, put aside with one hand the broad blue ribbon of her round straw hat, looked at me, smiled quietly, and again riveted her eyes on her book.

I pulled off my cap, and after fidgeting about a while on one spot, I went away with a heavy heart. "*Que suis-je pour elle?*"—I thought (God knows why) in French.

Familiar footsteps resounded behind me; I glanced round and beheld my father advancing toward me with swift, rapid strides.

"Is that the young Princess?"—he asked me.

"Yes."

"Dost thou know her?"

"I saw her this morning at the Princess her mother's."

My father halted and, wheeling abruptly round on his heels, retraced his steps. As he came on a level with Zinaída he bowed courteously to her. She bowed to him in return, not without some surprise on her face, and lowered her book. I saw that she followed him with her eyes. My father always dressed very elegantly, originally and simply; but his figure had never seemed to me more graceful, never had his grey hat sat more handsomely on his curls, which were barely beginning to grow thin.

I was on the point of directing my course toward Zinaída, but she did not even look at me, but raised her book once more and walked away.

## VI

I spent the whole of that evening and the following day in a sort of gloomy stupor. I remember that I made an effort to work, and took up Kaidánoff; but in vain did the large-printed lines and pages of the famous text-book flit before my eyes. Ten times in succession I read the words: "Julius Cæsar was distinguished for military daring," without understanding a word, and I flung aside my book. Before dinner I pomaded my hair again, and again donned my frock-coat and neckerchief.

"What's that for?"—inquired my mother.—"Thou art not a student yet, and God knows whether thou wilt pass thy examination. And thy round-jacket was made not very long ago. Thou must not discard it!"

"There are to be guests,"—I whispered, almost in despair.

"What nonsense! What sort of guests are they?"

I was compelled to submit. I exchanged my coat for my round-jacket, but did not remove my neckerchief. The Princess and her daughter made their appearance half an hour before dinner; the old woman had thrown a yellow shawl over her green gown, with which I was familiar, and had donned an old-fashioned mob-cap with ribbons of a fiery hue. She immediately began to talk about her notes of hand, to sigh and to bewail her poverty, and to "importune," but did not stand in the least upon ceremony; and she took snuff noisily and fidgeted and wriggled in her chair as before. It never seemed to enter her head that she was a Princess. On the other hand, Zinaída bore herself very stiffly, almost haughtily, like a real young Princess. Cold impassivity and dignity had made their appearance on her countenance, and I did not recognise her,—did not recognise her looks or her smile, although in this new aspect she seemed to me very beautiful. She wore a thin barège gown with pale-blue figures; her hair fell in long curls along her cheeks, in the English fashion: this coiffure suited the cold expression of her face.

My father sat beside her during dinner, and with the exquisite and imperturbable courtesy which was characteristic of him, showed attention to his neighbour. He glanced at her from time to time, and she glanced at him now and then, but in such a strange, almost hostile, manner. Their conversation proceeded in French;—I remember that I was surprised at the purity of Zinaída's accent. The old Princess, as before, did not restrain herself in the slightest degree during dinner, but ate a great deal and praised the food. My mother evidently found her wearisome, and answered her with a sort of sad indifference; my father contracted his brows in a slight frown from time to time. My mother did not like Zinaída either.

"She's a haughty young sprig,"—she said the next day.— "And when one comes to think of it, what is there for her to be proud of?—*avec sa mine de grisette!*"

"Evidently, thou hast not seen any grisettes,"—my father remarked to her.

"Of course I haven't, God be thanked!... Only, how art thou capable of judging of them?"

Zinaída paid absolutely no attention whatever to me. Soon after dinner the old Princess began to take her leave.

"I shall rely upon your protection, Márya Nikoláevna and Piótr Vasílitch,"—she said, in a sing-song tone, to my father and mother.—"What is to be done! I have seen prosperous days, but they are gone. Here am I a Radiance,"—she added, with an unpleasant laugh,—"but what's the good of an honour when you've nothing to eat?"—My father bowed respectfully to her and escorted her to the door of the anteroom. I was standing there in my round-jacket, and staring at the floor, as though condemned to death. Zinaída's behaviour toward me had definitively annihilated me. What, then, was my amazement when, as she passed me, she whispered to me hastily, and with her former affectionate expression in her eyes:—"Come to us at eight o'clock, do you hear? without fail...." I merely threw my hands apart in amazement;—but she was already retreating, having thrown a white scarf over her head.

## VII

Precisely at eight o'clock I entered the tiny wing inhabited by the Princess, clad in my coat, and with my hair brushed up into a crest on top of my head. The old servant glared surlily at me, and rose reluctantly from his bench. Merry voices resounded in the drawing-room. I opened the door and retreated a pace in astonishment. In the middle of the room, on a chair, stood the young Princess, holding a man's hat in front of her; around the chair thronged five men. They were trying to dip their hands into the hat, but she kept raising it on high and shaking it violently. On catching sight of me she exclaimed:—

"Stay, stay!  Here's a new guest; he must be given a ticket,"—and springing lightly from the chair, she seized me by the lapel of my coat.—"Come along,"—said she;— "why do you stand there?  Messieurs, allow me to make you acquainted: this is Monsieur Voldemar, the son of our neighbour. And this,"—she added, turning to me, and point- ing to the visitors in turn,—"is Count Malévsky, Doctor Lúshin, the poet Maidánoff, retired Captain Nirmátzky, and Byelovzóroff the hussar, whom you have already seen. I beg that you will love and favour each other."

I was so confused that I did not even bow to any one; in Doctor Lúshin I recognised that same swarthy gentleman who had so ruthlessly put me to shame in the garden; the others were strangers to me.

"Count!"—pursued Zinaída,—"write a ticket for M'sieu Voldemar."

"That is unjust,"—returned the Count, with a slight accent,—a very handsome and foppishly-attired man, with a dark complexion, expressive brown eyes, a thin, white little nose, and a slender moustache over his tiny mouth.— "He has not been playing at forfeits with us."

"'Tis unjust,"—repeated Byelovzóroff and the gentleman who had been alluded to as the retired Captain,—a man of forty, horribly pockmarked, curly-haired as a negro, round-shouldered, bow-legged, and dressed in a military coat without epaulets, worn open on the breast.

"Write a ticket, I tell you,"—repeated the Princess.— "What sort of a rebellion is this? M'sieu Voldemar is with us for the first time, and to-day no law applies to him. No grumbling—write; I will have it so."

The Count shrugged his shoulders, but submissively bowing his head, he took a pen in his white, ring-decked hand, tore off a scrap of paper and began to write on it.

"Permit me at least to explain to M'sieu Voldemar what it is all about,"—began Lúshin, in a bantering tone;— "otherwise he will be utterly at a loss. You see, young man, we are playing at forfeits; the Princess must pay a fine, and the one who draws out the lucky ticket must kiss her hand. Do you understand what I have told you?"

I merely glanced at him and continued to stand as though in a fog, while the Princess again sprang upon the chair and again began to shake the hat. All reached up to her—I among the rest.

"Maidánoff,"—said the Princess to the tall young man with a gaunt face, tiny mole-like eyes and extremely long, black hair,—"you, as a poet, ought to be magnanimous and surrender your ticket to M'sieu Voldemar, so that he may have two chances instead of one."

But Maidánoff shook his head in refusal and tossed his hair. I put in my hand into the hat after all the rest, drew out and unfolded a ticket.... O Lord! what were my sensations when I beheld on it, "Kiss!"

"Kiss!"—I cried involuntarily.

"Bravo! He has won,"—chimed in the Princess.—"How delighted I am!"—She descended from the chair, and gazed into my eyes so clearly and sweetly that my heart fairly laughed with joy.—"And are you glad?"—she asked me.

"I?" ... I stammered.

"Sell me your ticket,"—suddenly blurted out Byelovzóroff, right in my ear.—"I'll give you one hundred rubles for it."

I replied to the hussar by such a wrathful look that Zinaída clapped her hands, and Lúshin cried:—"That's a gallant fellow!"

"But,"—he went on,—"in my capacity of master of ceremonies, I am bound to see that all the regulations are carried out. M'sieu Voldemar, get down on one knee. That is our rule."

Zinaída stood before me with her head bent a little to one side, as though the better to scrutinise me, and offered me her hand with dignity. Things grew dim before my eyes; I tried to get down on one knee, plumped down on both knees, and applied my lips to Zinaída's fingers in so awkward a manner that I scratched the tip of my nose slightly on her nails.

"Good!"—shouted Lúshin, and helped me to rise.

The game of forfeits continued. Zinaída placed me beside her. What penalties they did invent! Among other things, she had to impersonate a "statue"—and she selected as a pedestal the monstrously homely Nirmátzky, ordering him to lie flat on the floor, and to tuck his face into his breast. The laughter did not cease for a single moment. All this noise and uproar, this unceremonious, almost tumultuous merriment, these unprecedented relations with strangers, fairly flew to my head; for I was a boy who had been reared soberly, and in solitude, and had grown up in a stately home of gentry. I became simply intoxicated, as though with wine. I began to shout with laughter and chatter more loudly than the rest, so that even the old Princess, who was sitting in the adjoining room with some sort of pettifogger from the Íversky Gate[4] who had been summoned for a conference, came out to take a look at me. But I felt so happy that, as the saying is, I didn't care a farthing for anybody's ridicule, or anybody's oblique glances.

Zinaída continued to display a preference for me and never let me leave her side. In one forfeit I was made to sit by her, covered up with one and the same silk kerchief: I was bound to tell her *my secret*. I remember how our two heads found themselves suddenly in choking, semi-transparent, fragrant gloom; how near and softly her eyes sparkled in that gloom, and how hotly her parted lips breathed; and her teeth were visible, and the tips of her hair tickled and burned me. I maintained silence. She smiled mysteriously and slyly, and at last whispered to me: "Well, what is it?" But I merely flushed and laughed, and turned away, and could hardly draw my breath. We got tired of forfeits, and

---

[4]The famous gate from the "White town" into the "China town," in Moscow, where there is a renowned holy picture of the Iberian Virgin, in a chapel. Evidently the lawyers' quarter was in this vicinity.—Translator.

began to play "string." Good heavens! what rapture I felt when, forgetting myself with gaping, I received from her a strong, sharp rap on my fingers; and how afterward I tried to pretend that I was yawning with inattention, but she mocked at me and did not touch my hands, which were awaiting the blow!

But what a lot of other pranks we played that same evening! We played on the piano, and sang, and danced, and represented a gipsy camp. We dressed Nirmátzky up like a bear, and fed him with water and salt. Count Malévsky showed us several card tricks, and ended by stacking the cards and dealing himself all the trumps at whist; upon which Lúshin "had the honour of congratulating him." Maidánoff declaimed to us fragments from his poem, "The Murderer" (this occurred in the very thick of romanticism), which he intended to publish in a black binding, with the title in letters of the colour of blood. We stole his hat from the knees of the pettifogger from the Íversky Gate, and made him dance the kazák dance by way of redeeming it. We dressed old Vonifáty up in a mob-cap, and the young Princess put on a man's hat.... It is impossible to recount all we did. Byelovzóroff alone remained most of the time in a corner, angry and frowning.... Sometimes his eyes became suffused with blood, he grew scarlet all over and seemed to be on the very point of swooping down upon all of us and scattering us on all sides, like chips; but the Princess glanced at him, menaced him with her finger, and again he retired into his corner.

We were completely exhausted at last. The old Princess was equal to anything, as she put it,—no shouts disconcerted her,—but she felt tired and wished to rest. At midnight supper was served, consisting of a bit of old, dry cheese and a few cold patties filled with minced ham, which seemed to us more savoury than any pasty; there was only one bottle of wine, and that was rather queer:—dark, with a swollen neck, and the wine in it left an after-taste of pinkish dye; however, no one drank it. Weary and happy to exhaustion, I emerged from the wing; a thunder-storm seemed to be brewing; the black storm-clouds grew larger and crept across the sky, visibly altering their smoky outlines. A light breeze was uneasily quivering in the dark trees, and somewhere beyond the horizon the thunder was growling angrily and dully, as though to itself.

I made my way through the back door to my room. My nurse-valet was sleeping on the floor and I was obliged to step over him; he woke up, saw me, and reported that my mother was angry with me, and had wanted to send after me again, but that my father had restrained her. I never went to bed without having bidden my mother good night and begged her blessing. There was no help for it! I told my valet that I would undress myself and go to bed unaided,— and extinguished the candle. But I did not undress and I did not go to bed.

I seated myself on a chair and sat there for a long time, as though enchanted. That which I felt was so new and so sweet.... I sat there, hardly looking around me and without moving, breathing slowly, and only laughing silently now, as I recalled, now inwardly turning cold at the thought that I was in love, that here it was, that love. Zinaída's face floated softly before me in the darkness—floated, but did not float away; her lips still smiled as mysteriously as ever, her eyes gazed somewhat askance at me, interrogatively, thoughtfully and tenderly ... as at the moment when I had parted from her. At last I rose on tiptoe, stepped to my bed and cautiously, without undressing, laid my head on the pillow, as though endeavouring by the sharp movement to frighten off that wherewith I was filled to overflowing....

I lay down, but did not even close an eye. I speedily perceived that certain faint reflections kept constantly falling into my room.... I raised myself and looked out of the window. Its frame was distinctly defined from the mysteriously and confusedly whitened panes. "'Tis the thunder-storm,"— I thought,—and so, in fact, there was a thunder-storm; but it had passed very far away, so that even the claps of thunder were not audible; only in the sky long, indistinct, branching flashes of lightning, as it were, were uninterruptedly flashing up. They were not flashing up so much as they were quivering and twitching, like the wing of a dying bird. I rose, went to the window, and stood there until morning.... The lightning-flashes never ceased for a moment; it was what is called a pitch-black night. I gazed at the dumb, sandy plain, at the dark mass of the Neskútchny Park, at the yellowish façades of the distant buildings, which also seemed to be trembling at every faint flash.... I gazed, and could not tear myself away; those dumb lightning-flashes, those restrained gleams, seemed to be responding to the dumb and secret outbursts which were flaring up within me also. Morning began to break; the dawn started forth in scarlet patches. With the approach of the sun the lightning-flashes grew paler and paler; they quivered more and more infrequently, and vanished at last, drowned in the sobering and unequivocal light of the breaking day.

And my lightning-flashes vanished within me also. I felt great fatigue and tranquillity ... but Zinaída's image continued to hover triumphantly over my soul. Only it, that image, seemed calm; like a flying swan from the marshy sedges, it separated itself from the other ignoble figures which surrounded it, and as I fell asleep, I bowed down before it for the last time in farewell and confiding adoration....

Oh, gentle emotions, soft sounds, kindness and calming of the deeply-moved soul, melting joy of the first feelings of love,—where are ye, where are ye?

## VIII

On the following morning, when I went down-stairs to tea, my mother scolded me,—although less than I had anticipated,—and made me narrate how I had spent the preceding evening. I answered her in few words, omitting many particulars and endeavouring to impart to my narrative the most innocent of aspects.

"Nevertheless, they are not people *comme il faut*,"— remarked my mother;—"and I do not wish thee to run after them, instead of preparing thyself for the examination, and occupying thyself."

As I knew that my mother's anxiety was confined to these few words, I did not consider it necessary to make her any reply; but after tea my father linked his arm in mine, and betaking himself to the garden with me, made me tell him everything I had done and seen at the Zasyékins'.

My father possessed a strange influence over me, and

our relations were strange. He paid hardly any attention to my education, but he never wounded me; he respected my liberty—he was even, if I may so express it, courteous to me ... only, he did not allow me to get close to him. I loved him, I admired him; he seemed to me a model man; and great heavens! how passionately attached to him I should have been, had I not constantly felt his hand warding me off! On the other hand, when he wished, he understood how to evoke in me, instantaneously, with one word, one movement, unbounded confidence in him. My soul opened, I chatted with him as with an intelligent friend, as with an indulgent preceptor ... then, with equal suddenness, he abandoned me, and again his hand repulsed me, caressingly and softly, but repulsed nevertheless.

Sometimes a fit of mirth came over him, and then he was ready to frolic and play with me like a boy (he was fond of every sort of energetic bodily exercise); once—only once—did he caress me with so much tenderness that I came near bursting into tears.... But his mirth and tenderness also vanished without leaving a trace, and what had taken place between us gave me no hopes for the future; it was just as though I had seen it all in a dream. I used to stand and scrutinise his clever, handsome, brilliant face ... and my heart would begin to quiver, and my whole being would yearn toward him, ... and he would seem to feel what was going on within me, and would pat me on the cheek in passing—and either go away, or begin to occupy himself with something, or suddenly freeze all over,—as he alone knew how to freeze,—and I would immediately shrivel up and grow frigid also. His rare fits of affection

for me were never called forth by my speechless but in-
telligible entreaties; they always came upon him without
warning. When meditating, in after years, upon my father's
character, I came to the conclusion that he did not care for
me or for family life; he loved something different, and
enjoyed that other thing to the full. "Seize what thou canst
thyself, and do not give thyself into any one's power; the
whole art of life consists in belonging to one's self,"—he
said to me once. On another occasion I, in my capacity of a
young democrat, launched out in his presence into argu-
ments about liberty (he was what I called "kind" that day;
at such times one could say whatever one liked to him).—
"Liberty,"—he repeated,—"but dost thou know what can give
a man liberty?"

"What?"

"Will, his own will, and the power which it gives is better
than liberty. Learn to will, and thou wilt be free, and wilt
command."

My father wished, first of all and most of all, to enjoy
life—and he did enjoy life.... Perhaps he had a presentiment
that he was not fated long to take advantage of the "art" of
living: he died at the age of forty-two.

I described to my father in detail my visit to the Zasyékins. He listened to me half-attentively, half-abstractedly,
as he sat on the bench and drew figures on the sand with the
tip of his riding-whip. Now and then he laughed, glanced
at me in a brilliant, amused sort of way, and spurred me
on by brief questions and exclamations. At first I could not
bring myself even to utter Zinaída's name, but I could not
hold out, and began to laud her. My father still continued

to laugh. Then he became thoughtful, dropped his eyes and rose to his feet.

I recalled the fact that, as he came out of the house, he had given orders that his horse should be saddled. He was a capital rider, and knew much better how to tame the wildest horses than did Mr. Rarey.

"Shall I ride with thee, papa?"—I asked him.

"No,"—he replied, and his face assumed its habitual indifferently-caressing expression.—"Go alone, if thou wishest; but tell the coachman that I shall not go."

He turned his back on me and walked swiftly away. I followed him with my eyes, until he disappeared beyond the gate. I saw his hat moving along the fence; he went into the Zasyékins' house.

He remained with them no more than an hour, but immediately thereafter went off to town and did not return home until evening.

After dinner I went to the Zasyékins' myself. I found no one in the drawing-room but the old Princess. When she saw me, she scratched her head under her cap with the end of her knitting-needle, and suddenly asked me: would I copy a petition for her?

"With pleasure,"—I replied, and sat down on the edge of a chair.

"Only look out, and see that you make the letters as large as possible,"—said the Princess, handing me a sheet of paper scrawled over in a slovenly manner:—"and couldn't you do it to-day, my dear fellow?"

"I will copy it this very day, madam."

The door of the adjoining room opened a mere crack

and Zinaída's face showed itself in the aperture,—pale, thoughtful, with hair thrown carelessly back. She stared at me with her large, cold eyes, and softly shut the door.

"Zína,—hey there, Zína!"—said the old woman. Zinaída did not answer. I carried away the old woman's petition, and sat over it the whole evening.

## IX

My "passion" began with that day. I remember that I then felt something of that which a man must feel when he enters the service: I had already ceased to be a young lad; I was in love. I have said that my passion dated from that day; I might have added that my sufferings also dated from that day. I languished when absent from Zinaída; my mind would not work, everything fell from my hands; I thought intently of her for days together.... I languished ... but in her presence I was no more at ease. I was jealous, I recognised my insignificance, I stupidly sulked and stupidly fawned; and, nevertheless, an irresistible force drew me to her, and every time I stepped across the threshold of her room, it was with an involuntary thrill of happiness. Zinaída immediately divined that I had fallen in love with her, and I never thought of concealing the fact; she mocked at my passion, played tricks on me, petted and tormented me. It is sweet to be the sole source, the autocratic and irresponsible cause of the greatest joys and the profoundest woe to another person, and I was like soft wax in Zinaída's hands. However, I was not the only one who was in love with her; all the men who were in the habit of visiting her house were crazy over her, and she kept them all in a leash at her feet. It amused her to arouse in them now hopes, now fears, to twist them about at her caprice (she called it, "knocking people against one another"),—and they never thought of resisting, and willingly submitted to her. In all her vivacious and beautiful being there was a certain peculiarly bewitching mixture of guilefulness and heedlessness, of artificiality and simplicity, of tranquillity and playfulness; over everything she did or said, over her every movement, hovered a light, delicate charm, and an original, sparkling force made itself felt in everything. And her face was incessantly changing and sparkling also; it expressed almost simultaneously derision, pensiveness, and passion. The most varied emotions, light, fleeting as the shadows of the clouds on a sunny, windy day, kept flitting over her eyes and lips.

Every one of her adorers was necessary to her. Byelovzóroff, whom she sometimes called "my wild beast," and sometimes simply "my own," would gladly have flung himself into the fire for her; without trusting to his mental capacities and other merits, he kept proposing that he should marry her, and hinting that the others were merely talking idly. Maidánoff responded to the poetical chords of her soul: a rather cold man, as nearly all writers are, he assured her with intense force—and perhaps himself also—that he adored her. He sang her praises in interminable verses and read them to her with an unnatural and a genuine sort of enthusiasm. And she was interested in him and jeered lightly at him; she did not believe in him greatly, and after listening to his effusions she made him read Púshkin, in order, as she said, to purify the air. Lúshin, the sneering doctor, who was cynical in speech, knew her best of all and loved her best of all, although he abused her to her face and behind her back. She respected him, but would not let him go, and sometimes, with a peculiar, malicious pleasure, made him feel that he was in her hands. "I am a coquette, I am heartless, I have the nature of an actress," she said to him one day in my presence; "and 'tis well! So give me your hand and I will stick a pin into it, and you will feel ashamed before this young man, and it will hurt you; but nevertheless, Mr. Upright Man, you will be so good as to laugh." Lúshin flushed crimson, turned away and bit his lips, but ended by putting out his hand. She pricked it, and he actually did break out laughing ... and she laughed also, thrusting the pin in pretty deeply and gazing into his eyes while he vainly endeavoured to glance aside....

I understood least of all the relations existing between Zinaída and Count Malévsky. That he was handsome, adroit, and clever even I felt, but the presence in him of some false, dubious element, was palpable even to me, a lad of sixteen, and I was amazed that Zinaída did not notice it. But perhaps she did detect that false element and it did not repel her. An irregular education, strange acquaintances, the constant presence of her mother, the poverty and disorder in the house—all this, beginning with the very freedom which the young girl enjoyed, together with the consciousness of her own superiority to the people who surrounded her, had developed in her a certain half-scornful carelessness and lack of exaction. No matter what happened—whether Vonifáty came to report that there was no sugar, or some wretched bit of gossip came to light, or the visitors got into a quarrel among themselves, she merely shook her curls, and said: "Nonsense!"—and grieved very little over it.

On the contrary, all my blood would begin to seethe when Malévsky would approach her, swaying his body cunningly like a fox, lean elegantly over the back of her chair and begin to whisper in her ear with a conceited and challenging smile, while she would fold her arms on her breast, gaze attentively at him and smile also, shaking her head the while.

"What possesses you to receive Malévsky?"—I asked her one day.

"Why, he has such handsome eyes,"—she replied.—"But that is no business of yours."

"You are not to think that I am in love with him,"—she said to me on another occasion.—"No; I cannot love people upon whom I am forced to look down. I must have some one who can subdue me.... And I shall not hit upon such an one, for God is merciful! I shall not spare any one who falls into my paws—no, no!"

"Do you mean to say that you will never fall in love?"

"And how about you? Don't I love you?"—she said, tapping me on the nose with the tip of her glove.

Yes, Zinaída made great fun of me. For the space of three weeks I saw her every day; and what was there that she did not do to me! She came to us rarely, but I did not regret that; in our house she was converted into a young lady, a Princess,—and I avoided her. I was afraid of betraying myself to my mother; she was not at all well disposed toward Zinaída, and kept a disagreeable watch on us. I was not so much afraid of my father; he did not appear to notice me, and talked little with her, but that little in a peculiarly clever and significant manner. I ceased to work, to read; I even ceased to stroll about the environs and to ride on horseback. Like a beetle tied by the leg, I hovered incessantly around the beloved wing; I believe I would have liked to remain there forever ... but that was impossible. My mother grumbled at me, and sometimes Zinaída herself drove me out. On such occasions I shut myself up in my own room, or walked off to the very end of the garden, climbed upon the sound remnant of a tall stone hothouse, and dangling my legs over the wall, I sat there for hours and stared,—stared without seeing anything. White butterflies lazily flitted among the nettles beside me; an audacious sparrow perched not far off on the half-demolished red bricks and twittered in an irritating manner, incessantly twisting his whole body about and spreading out his tail; the still distrustful crows now and then emitted a caw, as they sat high, high above me on the naked crest of a birch-tree; the sun and the wind played softly through its sparse branches; the chiming of the bells, calm and melancholy, at the Don Monastery was wafted to me now and then,—and I sat on, gazing and listening, and became filled with a certain nameless sensation which embraced everything: sadness and joy, and a presentiment of the future, and the desire and the fear of life. But I understood nothing at the time of all that which was fermenting within me, or I would have called it all by one name, the name of Zinaída.

But Zinaída continued to play with me as a cat plays with a mouse. Now she coquetted with me, and I grew agitated and melted with emotion; now she repulsed me, and I dared not approach her, dared not look at her.

I remember that she was very cold toward me for several days in succession and I thoroughly quailed, and when I timidly ran to the wing to see them, I tried to keep near the old Princess, despite the fact that she was scolding and screaming a great deal just at that time: her affairs connected with her notes of hand were going badly, and she had also had two scenes with the police-captain of the precinct.

One day I was walking through the garden, past the familiar fence, when I caught sight of Zinaída. Propped up on both arms, she was sitting motionless on the grass. I tried to withdraw cautiously, but she suddenly raised her head and made an imperious sign to me. I became petrified on the spot; I did not understand her the first time. She repeated her sign. I immediately sprang over the fence and ran joyfully to her; but she stopped me with a look and pointed to the path a couple of paces from her. In my confusion, not knowing what to do, I knelt down on the edge of the path. She was so pale, such bitter grief, such profound weariness were revealed in her every feature, that my heart contracted within me, and I involuntarily murmured: "What is the matter with you?"

Zinaída put out her hand, plucked a blade of grass, bit it, and tossed it away as far as she could.

"Do you love me very much?"—she inquired suddenly.—"Yes?"

I made no answer,—and what answer was there for me to make?

"Yes,"—she repeated, gazing at me as before.—"It is so. They are the same eyes,"—she added, becoming pensive, and covering her face with her hands.—"Everything has become repulsive to me,"—she whispered;—"I would like to go to the end of the world; I cannot endure this, I cannot reconcile myself.... And what is in store for me?... Akh, I am heavy at heart ... my God, how heavy at heart!"

"Why?"—I timidly inquired.

Zinaída did not answer me and merely shrugged her shoulders. I continued to kneel and to gaze at her with profound melancholy. Every word of hers fairly cut me to the heart. At that moment, I think I would willingly have given my life to keep her from grieving. I gazed at her, and nevertheless, not understanding why she was heavy at heart, I vividly pictured to myself how, in a fit of uncontrollable sorrow, she had suddenly gone into the garden, and had fallen on the earth, as though she had been mowed down. All around was bright and green; the breeze was rustling in the foliage of the trees, now and then rocking a branch of raspberry over Zinaída's head. Doves were cooing somewhere and the bees were humming as they flew low over the scanty grass. Overhead the sky shone blue,—but I was so sad....

"Recite some poetry to me,"—said Zinaída in a low voice, leaning on her elbow.—"I like to hear you recite verses. You make them go in a sing-song, but that does not matter, it is youthful. Recite to me: 'On the Hills of Georgia.'—Only, sit down first."

I sat down and recited, "On the Hills of Georgia."

"'That it is impossible not to love,'"—repeated Zinaída.—"That is why poetry is so nice; it says to us that which does not exist, and which is not only better than what does exist, but even more like the truth.... 'That it is impossible not to love'?—I would like to, but cannot!"—Again she fell silent for a space, then suddenly started and rose to her feet.— "Come along. Maidánoff is sitting with mamma; he brought his poem to me, but I left him. He also is embittered now ... how can it be helped? Some day you will find out ... but you must not be angry with me!"

Zinaída hastily squeezed my hand, and ran on ahead. We returned to the wing. Maidánoff set to reading us his poem of "The Murderer," which had only just been printed, but I did not listen. He shrieked out his four-footed iambics in a sing-song voice; the rhymes alternated and jingled like sleigh-bells, hollow and loud; but I kept staring all the while at Zinaída, and striving to understand the meaning of her strange words.

"Or, perchance, a secret rival
Has unexpectedly subjugated thee?"

suddenly exclaimed Maidánoff through his nose—and my eyes and Zinaída's met. She dropped hers and blushed faintly. I saw that she was blushing, and turned cold with fright. I had been jealous before, but only at that moment did the thought that she had fallen in love flash through my mind. "My God! She is in love!"

# X

My real tortures began from that moment. I cudgelled my brains, I pondered and pondered again, and watched Zinaída importunately, but secretly, as far as possible. A change had taken place in her, that was evident. She took to going off alone to walk, and walked a long while. Sometimes she did not show herself to her visitors; she sat for hours together in her chamber. This had not been her habit hitherto. Suddenly I became—or it seemed to me that I became—extremely penetrating. "Is it he? Or is it not he?"— I asked myself, as in trepidation I mentally ran from one of her admirers to another. Count Malévsky (although I felt ashamed to admit it for Zinaída's sake) privately seemed to me more dangerous than the others.

My powers of observation extended no further than the end of my own nose, and my dissimulation probably failed to deceive any one; at all events, Doctor Lúshin speedily saw through me. Moreover, he also had undergone a change of late; he had grown thin, he laughed as frequently as ever, but somehow it was in a duller, more spiteful, a briefer way;—an involuntary, nervous irritability had replaced his former light irony and feigned cynicism.

"Why are you forever tagging on here, young man?"— he said to me one day, when he was left alone with me in the Zasyékins' drawing-room. (The young Princess had not yet returned from her stroll and the shrill voice of the old Princess was resounding in the upper story; she was wrangling with her maid.)—"You ought to be studying your lessons, working while you are young;—but instead of that, what are you doing?"

"You cannot tell whether I work at home,"—I retorted not without arrogance, but also not without confusion.

"Much work you do! That's not what you have in your head. Well, I will not dispute ... at your age, that is in the natural order of things. But your choice is far from a happy one. Can't you see what sort of a house this is?"

"I do not understand you,"—I remarked.

"You don't understand me? So much the worse for you. I regard it as my duty to warn you. Fellows like me, old bachelors, may sit here: what harm will it do us? We are a hardened lot. You can't pierce our hide, but your skin is still tender; the air here is injurious for you,—believe me, you may become infected."

"How so?"

"Because you may. Are you healthy now? Are you in a normal condition? Is what you are feeling useful to you, good for you?"

"But what am I feeling?"—said I;—and in my secret soul I admitted that the doctor was right.

"Eh, young man, young man,"—pursued the doctor, with an expression as though something extremely insulting to me were contained in those two words;—"there's no use in your dissimulating, for what you have in your soul you still show in your face, thank God! But what's the use of arguing? I would not come hither myself, if ..." (the doctor set his teeth) ... "if I were not such an eccentric fellow. Only this is what amazes me—how you, with your intelligence, can fail to see what is going on around you."

"But what is going on?"—I interposed, pricking up my ears.

The doctor looked at me with a sort of sneering compassion.

"A nice person I am,"—said he, as though speaking to himself.—"What possessed me to say that to him. In a word,"—he added, raising his voice,—"I repeat to you: the atmosphere here is not good for you. You find it pleasant here, and no wonder! And the scent of a hothouse is pleasant also—but one cannot live in it! Hey! hearken to me,—set to work again on Kaidánoff."

The old Princess entered and began to complain to the doctor of toothache. Then Zinaída made her appearance.

"Here,"—added the old Princess,—"scold her, doctor, do. She drinks iced water all day long; is that healthy for her, with her weak chest?"

"Why do you do that?"—inquired Lúshin.

"But what result can it have?"

"What result? You may take cold and die."

"Really? Is it possible? Well, all right—that just suits me!"

"You don't say so!"—growled the doctor. The old Princess went away.

"I do say so,"—retorted Zinaída.—"Is living such a cheerful thing? Look about you.... Well—is it nice? Or do you think that I do not understand it, do not feel it? It affords me pleasure to drink iced water, and you can seriously assure me that such a life is worth too much for me to imperil it for a moment's pleasure—I do not speak of happiness."

"Well, yes,"—remarked Lúshin:—"caprice and independence.... Those two words sum you up completely; your whole nature lies in those two words."

Zinaída burst into a nervous laugh.

"You're too late by one mail, my dear doctor. You observe badly; you are falling behind.—Put on your spectacles.—I am in no mood for caprices now; how jolly to play pranks on you or on myself!—and as for independence.... M'sieu Voldemar,"—added Zinaída, suddenly stamping her foot,—"don't wear a melancholy face. I cannot endure to have people commiserating me."—She hastily withdrew.

"This atmosphere is injurious, injurious to you, young man,"—said Lúshin to me once more.

## XI

On the evening of that same day the customary visitors assembled at the Zasyékins'; I was among the number.

The conversation turned on Maidánoff's poem; Zinaída candidly praised it.—"But do you know what?"—she said:— "If I were a poet, I would select other subjects. Perhaps this is all nonsense, but strange thoughts sometimes come into my head, especially when I am wakeful toward morning, when the sky is beginning to turn pink and grey.—I would, for example.... You will not laugh at me?"

"No! No!"—we all exclaimed with one voice.

"I would depict,"—she went on, crossing her arms on her breast, and turning her eyes aside,—"a whole company of young girls, by night, in a big boat, on a tranquil river. The moon is shining, and they are all in white and wear garlands of white flowers, and they are singing, you know, something in the nature of a hymn."

"I understand, I understand, go on,"—said Maidánoff significantly and dreamily.

"Suddenly there is a noise—laughter, torches, tambourines on the shore.... It is a throng of bacchantes running with songs and outcries. It is your business to draw the picture, Mr. Poet ... only I would like to have the torches red and very smoky, and that the eyes of the bacchantes should gleam beneath their wreaths, and that the wreaths should be dark. Don't forget also tiger-skins and cups—and gold, a great deal of gold."

"But where is the gold to be?" inquired Maidánoff, tossing back his lank hair and inflating his nostrils.

"Where? On the shoulders, the hands, the feet, everywhere. They say that in ancient times women wore golden rings on their ankles.—The bacchantes call the young girls in the boat to come to them. The girls have ceased to chant their hymn,—they cannot go on with it,—but they do not stir; the river drifts them to the shore. And now suddenly one of them rises quietly.... This must be well described: how she rises quietly in the moonlight, and how startled her companions are.... She has stepped over the edge of the boat, the bacchantes have surrounded her, they have dashed off into the night, into the gloom.... Present at this point smoke in clouds; and everything has become thoroughly confused. Nothing is to be heard but their whimpering, and her wreath has been left lying on the shore."

Zinaída ceased speaking. "Oh, she is in love!"—I thought again.

"Is that all?"—asked Maidánoff.

"That is all,"—she replied.

"That cannot be made the subject of an entire poem,"—he remarked pompously,—"but I will utilise your idea for some lyrical verses."

"In the romantic vein?"—asked Malévsky.

"Of course, in the romantic vein—in Byron's style."

"But in my opinion, Hugo is better than Byron,"—remarked the young Count, carelessly:—"he is more interesting."

"Hugo is a writer of the first class,"—rejoined Maidánoff,

"and my friend Tonkoshéeff, in his Spanish romance, 'El Trovador'...."

"Ah, that's the book with the question-marks turned upside down?"—interrupted Zinaída.

"Yes. That is the accepted custom among the Spaniards. I was about to say that Tonkoshéeff...."

"Come now! You will begin to wrangle again about classicism and romanticism,"—Zinaída interrupted him again.— "Let us rather play...."

"At forfeits?"—put in Lúshin.

"No, forfeits is tiresome; but at comparisons." (This game had been invented by Zinaída herself; some object was named, and each person tried to compare it with something or other, and the one who matched the thing with the best comparison received a prize.) She went to the window. The sun had just set; long, crimson clouds hung high aloft in the sky.

"What are those clouds like?"—inquired Zinaída and, without waiting for our answers, she said:—"I think that they resemble those crimson sails which were on Cleopatra's golden ship, when she went to meet Antony. You were telling me about that not long ago, do you remember, Maidánoff?"

All of us, like Polonius in "Hamlet," decided that the clouds reminded us precisely of those sails, and that none of us could find a better comparison.

"And how old was Antony at that time?"—asked Zinaída.

"He was assuredly still a young man,"—remarked Malévsky.

"Yes, he was young,"—assented Maidánoff confidently.

"Excuse me,"—exclaimed Lúshin,—"he was over forty years of age."

"Over forty years of age,"—repeated Zinaída, darting a swift glance at him....

I soon went home.—"She is in love," my lips whispered involuntarily.... "But with whom?"

## XII

The days passed by. Zinaída grew more and more strange, more and more incomprehensible. One day I entered her house and found her sitting on a straw-bottomed chair, with her head pressed against the sharp edge of a table. She straightened up ... her face was again all bathed in tears.

"Ah! It's you!"—she said, with a harsh grimace.—"Come hither."

I went up to her: she laid her hand on my head and, suddenly seizing me by the hair, began to pull it.

"It hurts" ... I said at last.

"Ah! It hurts! And doesn't it hurt me? Doesn't it hurt me?"—she repeated.

"Aï!"—she suddenly cried, perceiving that she had pulled out a small tuft of my hair.—"What have I done? Poor M'sieu Voldemar!" She carefully straightened out the hairs she had plucked out, wound them round her finger, and twisted them into a ring.

"I will put your hair in my locket and wear it,"—she said, and tears glistened in her eyes.—"Perhaps that will comfort you a little ... but now, good-bye."

I returned home and found an unpleasant state of things there. A scene was in progress between my father and my mother; she was upbraiding him for something or other, while he, according to his wont, was maintaining a cold, polite silence—and speedily went away. I could not hear what my mother was talking about, neither did I care to know: I remember only, that, at the conclusion of the scene, she ordered me to be called to her boudoir, and expressed herself with great dissatisfaction about my frequent visits at the house of the old Princess, who was, according to her assertions, *une femme capable de tout*. I kissed her hand (I always did that when I wanted to put an end to the conversation), and went off to my own room. Zinaída's tears had completely discomfited me; I positively did not know what to think, and was ready to cry myself: I was still a child, in spite of my sixteen years. I thought no more of Malévsky, although Byelovzóroff became more and more menacing every day, and glared at the shifty Count like a wolf at a sheep; but I was not thinking of anything or of anybody. I lost myself in conjectures and kept seeking isolated spots. I took a special fancy to the ruins of the hothouse. I could clamber up on the high wall, seat myself, and sit there such an unhappy, lonely, and sad youth that I felt sorry for myself—and how delightful those mournful sensations were, how I gloated over them!...

One day, I was sitting thus on the wall, gazing off into the distance and listening to the chiming of the bells ... when suddenly something ran over me—not a breeze exactly, not a shiver, but something resembling a breath, the consciousness of some one's proximity.... I dropped my eyes. Below me, in a light grey gown, with a pink parasol on her shoulder, Zinaída was walking hastily along the road. She saw me, halted, and, pushing up the brim of her straw hat, raised her velvety eyes to mine.

"What are you doing there, on such a height?"—she asked me, with a strange sort of smile.—"There now,"—she went on,—"you are always declaring that you love me—jump down to me here on the road if you really do love me."

Before the words were well out of Zinaída's mouth I had flown down, exactly as though some one had given me a push from behind. The wall was about two fathoms high. I landed on the ground with my feet, but the shock was so violent that I could not retain my balance; I fell, and lost consciousness for a moment. When I came to myself I felt, without opening my eyes, that Zinaída was by my side.— "My dear boy,"—she was saying, as she bent over me—and tender anxiety was audible in her voice—"how couldst thou do that, how couldst thou obey?... I love thee ... rise."

Her breast was heaving beside me, her hands were touching my head, and suddenly—what were my sensations then!— her soft, fresh lips began to cover my whole face with kisses ... they touched my lips.... But at this point Zinaída probably divined from the expression of my face that I had already recovered consciousness, although I still did not open my eyes—and swiftly rising to her feet, she said:—"Come, get up, you rogue, you foolish fellow! Why do you lie there in the dust?"—I got up.

"Give me my parasol,"—said Zinaída.—"I have thrown it somewhere; and don't look at me like that what nonsense is this? You are hurt? You have burned yourself with the nettles, I suppose. Don't look at me like that, I tell you.... Why, he understands nothing, he doesn't answer me,"—she added, as though speaking to herself.... "Go home, M'sieu Voldemar, brush yourself off, and don't dare to follow me— if you do I shall be very angry, and I shall never again...."

She did not finish her speech and walked briskly away, while I sat down by the roadside ... my legs would not support me. The nettles had stung my hands, my back ached, and my head was reeling; but the sensation of beatitude which I then experienced has never since been repeated in my life. It hung like a sweet pain in all my limbs and broke out at last in rapturous leaps and exclamations. As a matter of fact, I was still a child.

## XIII

I was so happy and proud all that day; I preserved so vividly on my visage the feeling of Zinaída's kisses; I recalled her every word with such ecstasy; I so cherished my unexpected happiness that I even became frightened; I did not even wish to see her who was the cause of those new sensations. It seemed to me that I could ask nothing more of Fate, that now I must "take and draw a deep breath for the last time, and die." On the other hand, when I set off for the wing next day, I felt a great agitation, which I vainly endeavoured to conceal beneath the discreet facial ease suitable for a man who wishes to let it be understood that he knows how to keep a secret. Zinaída received me very simply, without any emotion, merely shaking her finger at me and asking: Had I any bruises? All my discreet ease of manner and mysteriousness instantly disappeared, and along with them my agitation. Of course I had not expected anything in particular, but Zinaída's composure acted on me like a dash

of cold water. I understood that I was a child in her eyes—
and my heart waxed very heavy! Zinaída paced to and fro
in the room, smiling swiftly every time she glanced at me;
but her thoughts were far away, I saw that clearly.... "Shall I
allude to what happened yesterday myself,"—I thought;—
"shall I ask her where she was going in such haste, in order
to find out, definitively?" ... but I merely waved my hand in
despair and sat down in a corner.

Byelovzóroff entered; I was delighted to see him.

"I have not found you a gentle saddle-horse,"—he began
in a surly tone;—"Freitag vouches to me for one—but I am
not convinced. I am afraid."

"Of what are you afraid, allow me to inquire?" asked
Zinaída.

"Of what? Why, you don't know how to ride. God forbid
that any accident should happen! And what has put that
freak into your head?"

"Come, that's my affair, M'sieu my wild beast. In that
case, I will ask Piótr Vasílievitch".... (My father was called
Piótr Vasílievitch.... I was amazed that she should mention
his name so lightly and freely, exactly as though she were
convinced of his readiness to serve her.)

"You don't say so!"—retorted Byelovzóroff.—"Is it with
him that you wish to ride?"

"With him or some one else,—that makes no difference
to you. Only not with you."

"Not with me,"—said Byelovzóroff.—"As you like. What
does it matter? I will get you the horse."

"But see to it that it is not a cow-like beast. I warn you in
advance that I mean to gallop."

"Gallop, if you wish.... But is it with Malévsky that you are going to ride?"

"And why shouldn't I ride with him, warrior? Come, quiet down. I'll take you too. You know that for me Malévsky is now—fie!"—She shook her head.

"You say that just to console me,"—growled Byelovzóroff.

Zinaída narrowed her eyes.—"Does that console you? oh ... oh oh ... warrior!"—she said at last, as though unable to find any other word.—"And would you like to ride with us, M'sieu Voldemar?"

"I'm not fond of riding ... in a large party," ... I muttered, without raising my eyes.

"You prefer a *tête-à-tête*?... Well, every one to his taste,"—she said, with a sigh.—"But go, Byelovzóroff, make an effort. I want the horse for to-morrow."

"Yes; but where am I to get the money?"—interposed the old Princess.

Zinaída frowned.

"I am not asking any from you; Byelovzóroff will trust me."

"He will, he will," grumbled the old Princess—and suddenly screamed at the top of her voice:—"Dunyáshka!"

"*Maman*, I made you a present of a bell,"—remarked the young Princess.

"Dunyáshka!"—repeated the old woman.

Byelovzóroff bowed himself out; I went out with him. Zinaída did not detain me.

## XIV

I rose early the next morning, cut myself a staff, and went off beyond the city barrier. "I'll have a walk and banish my grief,"—I said to myself. It was a beautiful day, brilliant but not too hot; a cheerful, fresh breeze was blowing over the earth and rustling and playing moderately, keeping in constant motion and agitating nothing. For a long time I roamed about on the hills and in the forests. I did not feel happy; I had left home with the intention of surrendering myself to melancholy;—but youth, the fine weather, the fresh air, the diversion of brisk pedestrian exercise, the delight of lying in solitude on the thick grass, produced their effect; the memory of those unforgettable words, of those kisses, again thrust themselves into my soul. It was pleasant to me to think that Zinaída could not, nevertheless, fail to do justice to my decision, to my heroism.... "Others are better for her than I,"—I thought:—"so be it! On the other hand, the others only say what they will do, but I have done it! And what else am I capable of doing for her?"—My imagination began to ferment. I began to picture to myself how I would save her from the hands of enemies; how, all bathed in blood, I would wrest her out of prison; how I would die at her feet. I recalled a picture which hung in our drawing-room of Malek-Adel carrying off Matilda— and thereupon became engrossed in the appearance of a big, speckled woodpecker which was busily ascending the slender trunk of a birch-tree, and uneasily peering out from behind it, now on the right, now on the left, like a musician from behind the neck of his bass-viol.

Then I began to sing: "Not the white snows,"—and ran off

into the romance which was well known at that period, "I will await thee when the playful breeze"; then I began to recite aloud Ermák's invocation to the stars in Khomyakóff's tragedy; I tried to compose something in a sentimental vein; I even thought out the line wherewith the whole poem was to conclude: "Oh, Zinaída! Zinaída!"—But it came to nothing. Meanwhile, dinner-time was approaching. I descended into the valley; a narrow, sandy path wound through it and led toward the town. I strolled along that path.... The dull trampling of horses' hoofs resounded behind me. I glanced round, involuntarily came to a standstill and pulled off my cap. I beheld my father and Zinaída. They were riding side by side. My father was saying something to her, bending his whole body toward her, and resting his hand on the neck of her horse; he was smiling. Zinaída was listening to him in silence, with her eyes severely downcast and lips compressed. At first I saw only them; it was not until several moments later that Byelovzóroff made his appearance from round a turn in the valley, dressed in hussar uniform with pelisse, and mounted on a foam-flecked black horse. The good steed was tossing his head, snorting and curvetting; the rider was both reining him in and spurring him on. I stepped aside. My father gathered up his reins and moved away from Zinaída; she slowly raised her eyes to his—and both set off at a gallop.... Byelovzóroff dashed headlong after them with clanking sword. "He is as red as a crab,"—I thought,—"and she.... Why is she so pale? She has been riding the whole morning—and yet she is pale?"

I redoubled my pace and managed to reach home just before dinner. My father was already sitting, re-dressed, well-washed and fresh, beside my mother's arm-chair, and reading aloud to her in his even, sonorous voice, the feuilleton of the *Journal des Débats*; but my mother was listening to him inattentively and, on catching sight of me, inquired where I had been all day, adding, that she did not like to have me prowling about God only knew where and God only knew with whom. "But I have been walking alone,"—I was on the point of replying; but I glanced at my father and for some reason or other held my peace.

## XV

During the course of the next five or six days I hardly saw Zinaída; she gave it out that she was ill, which did not, however, prevent the habitual visitors from presenting themselves at the wing—"to take their turn in attendance,"—as they expressed it;—all except Maidánoff, who immediately became dispirited as soon as he had no opportunity to go into raptures. Byelovzóroff sat morosely in a corner, all tightly buttoned up and red in the face; on Count Malévsky's delicate visage hovered constantly a sort of evil smile; he really had fallen into disfavour with Zinaída and listened with particular pains to the old Princess, and drove with her to the Governor-General's in a hired carriage. But this trip proved unsuccessful and even resulted in an unpleasantness for Malévsky: he was reminded of some row with certain Putéisk officers, and was compelled, in self-justification, to say that he was inexperienced at the time. Lúshin came twice a day, but did not remain long. I was somewhat afraid of him after our last explanation and, at the same time, I felt a sincere attachment for him. One day he went for a stroll with me in the Neskútchny Park, was very good-natured and amiable, imparted to me the names and properties of various plants and flowers, and suddenly exclaimed—without rhyme or reason, as the saying is—as he smote himself on the brow: "And I, like a fool, thought she was a coquette! Evidently, it is sweet to sacrifice one's self—for some people!"

"What do you mean to say by that?"—I asked.

"I don't mean to say anything to you,"—returned Lúshin, abruptly.

Zinaída avoided me; my appearance—I could not but perceive the fact—produced an unpleasant impression on her. She involuntarily turned away from me ... involuntarily; that was what was bitter, that was what broke my heart! But there was no help for it and I tried to keep out of her sight and only stand guard over her from a distance, in which I was not always successful. As before, something incomprehensible was taking place with her; her face had become different—she was altogether a different person. I was particularly struck by the change which had taken place in her on a certain warm, tranquil evening. I was sitting on a low bench under a wide-spreading elder-bush; I loved that little nook; the window of Zinaída's chamber was visible thence. I was sitting there; over my head, in the darkened foliage, a tiny bird was rummaging fussily about; a great cat with outstretched back had stolen into the garden, and the first beetles were booming heavily in the air, which was still transparent although no longer light. I sat there and stared at the window, and waited to see whether some one would not open it: and, in fact, it did open, and Zinaída made her appearance in it. She wore a white gown, and she herself—her face, her shoulders and her hands—was pale to whiteness. She remained for a long time motionless, and for a long time stared, without moving, straight in front of her from beneath her contracted brows. I did not recognise that look in her. Then she clasped her hands very, very tightly, raised them to her lips, to her forehead—and suddenly, unlocking her fingers, pushed her hair away from her ears, shook it back and, throwing her head downward from above with a certain decisiveness, she shut the window with a bang.

Two days later she met me in the park. I tried to step aside, but she stopped me.

"Give me your hand"—she said to me, with her former affection.—"It is a long time since you and I have had a chat."

I looked at her; her eyes were beaming softly and her face was smiling, as though athwart a mist.

"Are you still ailing?"—I asked her.

"No, everything has passed off now,"—she replied, breaking off a small, red rose.—"I am a little tired, but that will pass off also."

"And will you be once more the same as you used to be?"—I queried.

Zinaída raised the rose to her face, and it seemed to me as though the reflection of the brilliant petals fell upon her cheeks.—"Have I changed?"—she asked me.

"Yes, you have changed,"—I replied in a low voice.

"I was cold toward you,—I know that,"—began Zinaída;—"but you must not pay any heed to that.... I could not do

60

otherwise.... Come, what's the use of talking about that?"

"You do not want me to love you—that's what!" I exclaimed gloomily, with involuntary impetuosity.

"Yes, love me, but not as before."

"How then?"

"Let us be friends,—that is how!"—Zinaída allowed me to smell of the rose.—"Listen; I am much older than you, you know—I might be your aunt, really; well, if not your aunt, then your elder sister. While you...."

"I am a child to you,"—I interrupted her.

"Well, yes, you are a child, but a dear, good, clever child, of whom I am very fond. Do you know what? I will appoint you to the post of my page from this day forth; and you are not to forget that pages must not be separated from their mistress. Here is a token of your new dignity for you,"—she added, sticking the rose into the button-hole of my round-jacket; "a token of our favour toward you."

"I have received many favours from you in the past,"—I murmured.

"Ah!"—said Zinaída, and darting a sidelong glance at me.—"What a memory you have! Well? And I am ready now also...."

And bending toward me, she imprinted on my brow a pure, calm kiss.

I only stared at her—but she turned away and, saying,—"Follow me, my page,"—walked to the wing. I followed her—and was in a constant state of bewilderment.—"Is it possible,"—I thought,—"that this gentle, sensible young girl is that same Zinaída whom I used to know?"—And her very walk seemed to me more quiet, her whole figure more majestic, more graceful....

And, my God! with what fresh violence did love flame up within me!

## XVI

After dinner the visitors were assembled again in the wing, and the young Princess came out to them. The whole company was present, in full force, as on that first evening, never to be forgotten by me: even Nirmátzky had dragged himself thither. Maidánoff had arrived earlier than all the rest; he had brought some new verses. The game of forfeits began again, but this time without the strange sallies, without pranks and uproar; the gipsy element had vanished. Zinaída gave a new mood to our gathering. I sat beside her, as a page should. Among other things, she proposed that the one whose forfeit was drawn should narrate his dream; but this was not a success. The dreams turned out to be either uninteresting (Byelovzóroff had dreamed that he had fed his horse on carp, and that it had a wooden head), or unnatural, fictitious. Maidánoff regaled us with a complete novel; there were sepulchres and angels with harps, and burning lights and sounds wafted from afar. Zinaída did not allow him to finish. "If it is a question of invention,"—said she,—"then let each one relate something which is positively made up."—Byelovzóroff had to speak first.

The young hussar became confused.—"I cannot invent anything!"—he exclaimed.

"What nonsense!"—interposed Zinaída.—"Come, imagine, for instance, that you are married, and tell us how you would pass the time with your wife. Would you lock her up?"

"I would."

"And would you sit with her yourself?"

"I certainly would sit with her myself."

"Very good. Well, and what if that bored her, and she betrayed you?"

"I would kill her."

"Just so. Well, now supposing that I were your wife, what would you do then?"

Byelovzóroff made no answer for a while.—"I would kill myself...."

Zinaída burst out laughing.—"I see that there's not much to be got out of you."

The second forfeit fell to Zinaída's share. She raised her eyes to the ceiling and meditated.—"See here,"—she began at last,—"this is what I have devised.... Imagine to yourselves a magnificent palace, a summer night, and a marvellous ball. This ball is given by the young Queen. Everywhere there are gold, marble, silk, lights, diamonds, flowers, the smoke of incense—all the whims of luxury."

"Do you love luxury?"—interrupted Lúshin.

"Luxury is beautiful,"—she returned;—"I love everything that is beautiful."

"More than what is fine?"—he asked.

"That is difficult; somehow I don't understand. Don't bother me. So then, there is a magnificent ball. There are many guests, they are all young, very handsome, brave; all are desperately in love with the Queen."

"Are there no women among the guests?"—inquired Malévsky.

"No—or stay—yes, there are."

"Also very handsome?"

"Charming. But the men are all in love with the Queen. She is tall and slender; she wears a small gold diadem on her black hair."

I looked at Zinaída—and at that moment she seemed so far above us, her white forehead and her impassive eyebrows exhaled so much clear intelligence and such sovereignty, that I said to myself: "Thou thyself art that Queen!"

"All throng around her,"—pursued Zinaída;—"all lavish the most flattering speeches on her."

"And is she fond of flattery?"—asked Lúshin.

"How intolerable! He is continually interrupting.... Who does not like flattery?"

"One more final question,"—remarked Malévsky:—"Has the Queen a husband?"

"I have not thought about that. No, why should she have a husband?"

"Of course,"—assented Malévsky;—"why should she have a husband?"

"Silence!"—exclaimed, in English, Maidánoff, who spoke French badly.

"*Merci*,"—said Zinaída to him.—"So then, the Queen listens to those speeches, listens to the music, but does not look at a single one of the guests. Six windows are open from top to bottom, from ceiling to floor, and behind them are the dark sky with great stars and the dark garden with huge trees. The Queen gazes into the garden. There, near the trees is a fountain: it gleams white athwart the gloom—

long, as long as a spectre. The Queen hears the quiet plashing of its waters in the midst of the conversation and the music. She gazes and thinks: 'All of you gentlemen are noble, clever, wealthy; you are all ready to die at my feet, I rule over you; ... but yonder, by the side of the fountain, by the side of that plashing water, there is standing and waiting for me the man whom I love, who rules over me. He wears no rich garments, nor precious jewels; no one knows him; but he is waiting for me, and is convinced that I shall come—and I shall come, and there is no power in existence which can stop me when I wish to go to him and remain with him and lose myself with him yonder, in the gloom of the park, beneath the rustling of the trees, beneath the plashing of the fountain....'"

Zinaída ceased speaking.

"Is that an invention?"—asked Malévsky slyly.

Zinaída did not even glance at him.

"But what should we do, gentlemen,"—suddenly spoke up Lúshin,—"if we were among the guests and knew about that lucky man by the fountain?"

"Stay, stay,"—interposed Zinaída:—"I myself will tell you what each one of you would do. You, Byelovzóroff, would challenge him to a duel; you, Maidánoff, would write an epigram on him.... But no—you do not know how to write epigrams; you would compose a long iambic poem on him, after the style of Barbier, and would insert your production in the *Telegraph*. You, Nirmátzky, would borrow from him ... no, you would lend him money on interest; you, doctor...." She paused.... "I really do not know about you,—what you would do."

"In my capacity of Court-physician," replied Lúshin, "I would advise the Queen not to give balls when she did not feel in the mood for guests...."

"Perhaps you would be in the right. And you, Count?"

"And I?"—repeated Malévsky, with an evil smile.

"And you would offer him some poisoned sugar-plums."

Malévsky's face writhed a little and assumed for a moment a Jewish expression; but he immediately burst into a guffaw.

"As for you, M'sieu Voldemar...." went on Zinaída,—"but enough of this; let us play at some other game."

"M'sieu Voldemar, in his capacity of page to the Queen, would hold up her train when she ran off into the park,"—remarked Malévsky viciously.

I flared up, but Zinaída swiftly laid her hand on my shoulder and rising, said in a slightly tremulous voice:—"I have never given Your Radiance the right to be insolent, and therefore I beg that you will withdraw."—She pointed him to the door.

"Have mercy, Princess,"—mumbled Malévsky, turning pale all over.

"The Princess is right,"—exclaimed Byelovzóroff, rising to his feet also.

"By God! I never in the least expected this,"—went on Malévsky:—"I think there was nothing in my words which.... I had no intention of offending you.... Forgive me."

Zinaída surveyed him with a cold glance, and smiled coldly.—"Remain, if you like,"—she said, with a careless wave of her hand.—"M'sieu Voldemar and I have taken offence without cause. You find it merry to jest.... I wish you well."

"Forgive me,"—repeated Malévsky once more; and I, recalling Zinaída's movement, thought again that a real queen could not have ordered an insolent man out of the room with more majesty.

The game of forfeits did not continue long after this little scene; all felt somewhat awkward, not so much in consequence of the scene itself as from another, not entirely defined, but oppressive sensation. No one alluded to it, but each one was conscious of its existence within himself and in his neighbour. Maidánoff recited to us all his poems— and Malévsky lauded them with exaggerated warmth.

"How hard he is trying to appear amiable now,"—Lúshin whispered to me.

We soon dispersed. Zinaída had suddenly grown pensive; the old Princess sent word that she had a headache; Nirmátzky began to complain of his rheumatism....

For a long time I could not get to sleep; Zinaída's narrative had impressed me.—"Is it possible that it contains a hint?"—I asked myself:—"and at whom was she hinting? And if there really is some one to hint about ... what must I decide to do? No, no, it cannot be,"—I whispered, turning over from one burning cheek to the other.... But I called to mind the expression of Zinaída's face during her narration.... I called to mind the exclamation which had broken from Lúshin in the Neskútchny Park, the sudden changes in her treatment of me—and lost myself in conjectures. "Who is he?" Those three words seemed to stand in front of my eyes, outlined in the darkness; a low-lying, ominous cloud seemed to be hanging over me—and I felt its pressure—

and waited every moment for it to burst. I had grown used to many things of late; I had seen many things at the Za-syékins'; their disorderliness, tallow candle-ends, broken knives and forks, gloomy Vonifáty, the shabby maids, the manners of the old Princess herself,—all that strange life no longer surprised me.... But to that which I now dimly felt in Zinaída I could not get used.... "An adventuress,"—my mother had one day said concerning her. An adventuress—she, my idol, my divinity! That appellation seared me; I tried to escape from it by burrowing into my pillow; I raged—and at the same time, to what would not I have agreed, what would not I have given, if only I might be that happy mortal by the fountain!...

My blood grew hot and seethed within me. "A garden ... a fountain," ... I thought.... "I will go into the garden." I dressed myself quickly and slipped out of the house. The night was dark, the trees were barely whispering; a quiet chill was descending from the sky, an odour of fennel was wafted from the vegetable-garden. I made the round of all the alleys; the light sound of my footsteps both disconcerted me and gave me courage; I halted, waiting and listening to hear how my heart was beating quickly and violently. At last I approached the fence and leaned against a slender post. All at once—or was it only my imagination?—a woman's figure flitted past a few paces distant from me.... I strained my eyes intently on the darkness; I held my breath. What was this? Was it footsteps that I heard or was it the thumping of my heart again?—"Who is here?"—I stammered in barely audible tones. What was that again? A suppressed laugh?... or a rustling in the leaves?... or a sigh close to my very ear?

I was terrified.... "Who is here?"—I repeated, in a still lower voice.

The breeze began to flutter for a moment; a fiery band flashed across the sky; a star shot down.—"Is it Zinaída?"—I tried to ask, but the sound died on my lips. And suddenly everything became profoundly silent all around, as often happens in the middle of the night.... Even the katydids ceased to shrill in the trees; only a window rattled somewhere. I stood and stood, then returned to my chamber, to my cold bed. I felt a strange agitation—exactly as though I had gone to a tryst, and had remained alone, and had passed by some one else's happiness.

## XVII

The next day I caught only a glimpse of Zinaída; she drove away somewhere with the old Princess in a hired carriage. On the other hand, I saw Lúshin—who, however, barely deigned to bestow a greeting on me—and Malévsky. The young Count grinned and entered into conversation with me in friendly wise. Among all the visitors to the wing he alone had managed to effect an entrance to our house, and my mother had taken a fancy to him. My father did not favour him and treated him politely to the point of insult.

"Ah, *monsieur le page*,"—began Malévsky,—"I am very glad to meet you. What is your beauteous queen doing?"

His fresh, handsome face was so repulsive to me at that moment, and he looked at me with such a scornfully-playful stare, that I made him no answer whatsoever.

"Are you still in a bad humour?"—he went on.—"There is no occasion for it. It was not I, you know, who called you a page; and pages are chiefly with queens. But permit me to observe to you that you are fulfilling your duties badly."

"How so?"

"Pages ought to be inseparable from their sovereigns; pages ought to know everything that they do; they ought even to watch over them,"—he added, lowering his voice,—"day and night."

"What do you mean by that?"

"What do I mean? I think I have expressed myself plainly. Day—and night. It does not matter so much about the day; by day it is light and there are people about; but by night—that's exactly the time to expect a catastrophe. I advise you not to sleep o'nights and to watch, watch with all your might. Remember—in a garden, by night, near the fountain—that's where you must keep guard. You will thank me for this."

Malévsky laughed and turned his back on me. He did not, in all probability, attribute any special importance to what he had said to me; he bore the reputation of being a capital hand at mystification, and was renowned for his cleverness in fooling people at the masquerades, in which that almost unconscious disposition to lie, wherewith his whole being was permeated, greatly aided him.... He had merely wished to tease me; but every word of his trickled like poison through all my veins.—The blood flew to my head.

"Ah! so that's it!"—I said to myself:—"good! So it was not for nothing that I felt drawn to the garden! That shall not be!" I exclaimed, smiting myself on the breast with my fist; although I really did not know what it was that I was determined not to permit.—"Whether Malévsky himself comes into the garden,"—I thought (perhaps he had blurted out a secret; he was insolent enough for that),—"or some one else,"—(the fence of our vegetable-garden was very low and it cost no effort to climb over it)—"at any rate, it will be all the worse for the person whom I catch! I would not advise any one to encounter me! I'll show the whole world and her, the traitress,"—(I actually called her a traitress)—"that I know how to avenge myself!"

I returned to my own room, took out of my writing-table a recently purchased English knife, felt of the sharp blade, and, knitting my brows, thrust it into my pocket with a cold and concentrated decision, exactly as though it was nothing remarkable for me to do such deeds, and this was not the first occasion. My heart swelled angrily within me and grew stony; I did not unbend my brows until nightfall and did not relax my lips, and kept striding back and forth, clutching the knife which had grown warm in my pocket, and preparing myself in advance for something terrible. These new, unprecedented emotions so engrossed and even cheered me, that I thought very little about Zinaída herself. There kept constantly flitting through my head Aleko, the young gipsy:[5]—"Where art thou going, handsome youth?— Lie down...." and then: "Thou'rt all with blood bespattered!... Oh, what is't that thou hast done?... Nothing!" With what a harsh smile I repeated that: that "Nothing!"

My father was not at home; but my mother, who for some time past had been in a state of almost constant, dull irritation, noticed my baleful aspect at supper, and said to me:—"What art thou sulking at, like a mouse at groats?"—

---

[5]In Púshkin's poem, "The Gipsies."—Translator.

I merely smiled patronisingly at her by way of reply and thought to myself: "If they only knew!"—The clock struck eleven; I went to my own room but did not undress; I was waiting for midnight; at last it struck.—"'Tis time!"—I hissed between my teeth, and buttoning my coat to the throat and even turning up my sleeves I betook myself to the garden.

I had selected a place beforehand where I meant to stand on guard. At the end of the garden, at the spot where the fence, which separated our property from the Zasyékins', abutted on the party-wall, grew a solitary spruce-tree. Standing beneath its low, thick branches, I could see well, as far as the nocturnal gloom permitted, all that went on around; there also meandered a path which always seemed to me mysterious; like a serpent it wound under the fence, which at that point bore traces of clambering feet, and led to an arbour of dense acacias. I reached the spruce-tree, leaned against its trunk and began my watch.

The night was as tranquil as the preceding one had been; but there were fewer storm-clouds in the sky, and the outlines of the bushes, even of the tall flowers, were more plainly discernible. The first moments of waiting were wearisome, almost terrible. I had made up my mind to everything; I was merely considering how I ought to act. Ought I to thunder out: "Who goes there? Halt! Confess— or die!"—or simply smite.... Every sound, every noise and rustling seemed to me significant, unusual.... I made ready.... I bent forward.... But half an hour, an hour, elapsed; my blood quieted down and turned cold; the consciousness that I was doing all this in vain, that I was even somewhat ridiculous, that Malévsky had been making fun of me, began to steal into my soul. I abandoned my ambush and made the round of the entire garden. As though expressly, not the slightest sound was to be heard anywhere; everything was at rest; even our dog was asleep, curled up in a ball at the gate. I climbed up on the ruin of the hothouse, beheld before me the distant plain, recalled my meeting with Zinaída, and became immersed in meditation....

I started.... I thought I heard the creak of an opening door, then the light crackling of a broken twig. In two bounds I had descended from the ruin—and stood petrified on the spot. Swift, light but cautious footsteps were plainly audible in the garden. They were coming toward me. "Here he is.... Here he is, at last!"—darted through my heart. I convulsively jerked the knife out of my pocket, convulsively opened it—red sparks whirled before my eyes, the hair stood up on my head with fright and wrath.... The steps were coming straight toward me—I bent over, and went to meet them.... A man made his appearance.... My God! It was my father!

I recognised him instantly, although he was all enveloped in a dark cloak,—and had pulled his hat down over his face. He went past me on tiptoe. He did not notice me although nothing concealed me; but I had so contracted myself and shrunk together that I think I must have been on a level with the ground. The jealous Othello, prepared to murder, had suddenly been converted into the school-boy.... I was so frightened by the unexpected apparition of my father that I did not even take note, at first, in what direction he was going and where he had disappeared. I merely straightened up at the moment and thought: "Why is my father walking in the garden by night?"—when everything around had relapsed into silence. In my alarm I had dropped my knife in the grass, but I did not even try to find it; I felt very much ashamed. I became sobered on the instant. But as I wended my way home, I stepped up to my little bench under the elder-bush and cast a glance at the little window of Zinaída's chamber. The small, somewhat curved panes of the little window gleamed dully blue in the faint light which fell from the night sky. Suddenly their colour began to undergo a change.... Behind them—I saw it, saw it clearly,—a whitish shade was lowered, descended to the sill,—and there remained motionless.

"What is the meaning of that?"—I said aloud, almost involuntarily, when I again found myself in my own room.— "Was it a dream, an accident, or...." The surmises which suddenly came into my head were so new and strange that I dared not even yield to them.

## XVIII

I rose in the morning with a headache. My agitation of the night before had vanished. It had been replaced by an oppressive perplexity and a certain, hitherto unknown sadness,—exactly as though something had died in me.

"What makes you look like a rabbit which has had half of its brain removed?"—said Lúshin, who happened to meet me. At breakfast I kept casting covert glances now at my father, now at my mother; he was calm, as usual; she, as usual, was secretly irritated. I waited to see whether my father would address me in a friendly way, as he sometimes did.... But he did not even caress me with his cold, everyday affection.—"Shall I tell Zinaída all?"—I thought.... "For it makes no difference now—everything is over between us." I went to her, but I not only did not tell her anything,—I did not even get a chance to talk to her as I would have liked. The old Princess's son, a cadet aged twelve, had come from Petersburg to spend his vacation with her; Zinaída immediately confided her brother to me.—"Here, my dear Volódya,"—said she (she called me so for the first time), "is a comrade for you. His name is Volódya also. Pray, like him; he's a wild little fellow still, but he has a good heart. Show him Neskútchny Park, walk with him, take him under your protection. You will do that, will you not? You, too, are such a good fellow!"—She laid both hands affectionately on my shoulder—and I was reduced to utter confusion. The arrival of that boy turned me into a boy. I stared in silence at the cadet, who riveted his eyes in corresponding silence on me. Zinaída burst out laughing and pushed us toward each other.—"Come, embrace, children!"—We embraced.—"I'll take you into the garden if you wish,—shall I?"—I asked the cadet.

"Certainly, sir,"—he replied, in a hoarse, genuine cadet voice. Again Zinaída indulged in a burst of laughter.... I managed to notice that never before had she had such charming colour in her face. The cadet and I went off together. In our garden stood an old swing. I seated him on the thin little board and began to swing him. He sat motionless in his new little uniform of thick cloth with broad gold galloon, and clung tightly to the ropes.

"You had better unhook your collar,"—I said to him.

"Never mind, sir,[6] we are used to it, sir,"—he said, and cleared his throat.

He resembled his sister; his eyes were particularly suggestive of her. It was pleasant to me to be of service to him; and, at the same time, that aching pain kept quietly gnawing at my heart. "Now I really am a child," I thought; "but last night...." I remembered where I had dropped my knife and found it. The cadet asked me to lend it to him, plucked a thick stalk of lovage, cut a whistle from it, and began to pipe. Othello piped also.

But in the evening, on the other hand, how he did weep, that same Othello, over Zinaída's hands when, having sought him out in a corner of the garden, she asked him what made him so melancholy. My tears streamed with such violence that she was frightened.—"What is the matter with you? What is the matter with you, Volódya?"—she kept repeating, and seeing that I made her no reply, she took it into her head to kiss my wet cheek. But I turned away from her and whispered through my sobs:—"I know everything: why have you trifled with me?... Why did you want my love?"

"I am to blame toward you, Volódya" ... said Zinaída.— "Akh, I am very much to blame" ... she said, and clenched her hands.—"How much evil, dark, sinful, there is in me!... But I am not trifling with you now, I love you—you do not suspect why and how.... But what is it you know?"

What could I say to her? She stood before me and gazed at me—and I belonged to her wholly, from head to foot, as soon as she looked at me.... A quarter of an hour later I was running a race with the cadet and Zinaída; I was

<hr />

[6]The respectful "s," which is an abbreviation of "sir" or "madam."—Translator.

not weeping; I was laughing, although my swollen eyelids dropped tears from laughing; on my neck, in place of a tie, was bound a ribbon of Zinaída's, and I shouted with joy when I succeeded in seizing her round the waist. She did with me whatsoever she would.

## XIX

I should be hard put to it, if I were made to narrate in detail all that went on within me in the course of the week which followed my unsuccessful nocturnal expedition. It was a strange, feverish time, a sort of chaos in which the most opposite emotions, thoughts, suspicions, hopes, joys, and sufferings revolved in a whirlwind; I was afraid to look into myself, if a sixteen-year-old can look into himself; I was afraid to account to myself for anything whatsoever; I simply made haste to live through the day until the evening; on the other hand, at night I slept ... childish giddiness helped me. I did not want to know whether I was beloved, and would not admit to myself that I was not beloved; I shunned my father—but could not shun Zinaída.... I burned as with fire in her presence, ... but what was the use of my knowing what sort of fire it was wherewith I burned and melted—seeing that it was sweet to me to burn and melt! I surrendered myself entirely to my impressions, and dealt artfully with myself, turned away from my memories and shut my eyes to that of which I had a presentiment in the future.... This anguish probably would not have continued long ... a thunder-clap put an instantaneous end to everything and hurled me into a new course.

On returning home one day to dinner from a rather

long walk, I learned with surprise that I was to dine alone; that my father had gone away, while my mother was ill, did not wish to dine and had shut herself up in her bedroom. From the footmen's faces I divined that something unusual had taken place.... I dared not interrogate them, but I had a friend, the young butler Philípp, who was passionately fond of poetry and an artist on the guitar; I applied to him. From him I learned that a frightful scene had taken place between my father and mother (for in the maids' room everything was audible, to the last word; a great deal had been said in French, but the maid Másha had lived for five years with a dressmaker from Paris and understood it all); that my mother had accused my father of infidelity, of being intimate with the young lady our neighbour; that my father had first defended himself, then had flared up and in his turn had made some harsh remark "seemingly about her age," which had set my mother to crying; that my mother had also referred to a note of hand, which appeared to have been given to the old Princess, and expressed herself very vilely about her, and about the young lady as well; and that then my father had threatened her.—"And the whole trouble arose,"—pursued Philípp, "out of an anonymous letter; but who wrote it no one knows; otherwise there was no reason why this affair should have come out."

"But has there been anything?"—I enunciated with difficulty, while my hands and feet turned cold, and something began to quiver in the very depths of my breast.

Philípp winked significantly.—"There has. You can't conceal such doings, cautious as your papa has been in this case;—still, what possessed him, for example, to hire a carriage, or to ... for you can't get along without people there also."

I dismissed Philípp, and flung myself down on my bed. I did not sob, I did not give myself up to despair; I did not ask myself when and how all this had taken place; I was not surprised that I had not guessed it sooner, long before—I did not even murmur against my father.... That which I had learned was beyond my strength; this sudden discovery had crushed me.... All was over. All my flowers had been plucked up at one blow and lay strewn around me, scattered and trampled under foot.

## XX

On the following day my mother announced that she was going to remove to town. My father went into her bedroom in the morning and sat there a long time alone with her. No one heard what he said to her, but my mother did not weep any more; she calmed down and asked for something to eat, but did not show herself and did not alter her intention. I remember that I wandered about all day long, but did not go into the garden and did not glance even once at the wing—and in the evening I was the witness of an amazing occurrence; my father took Count Malévsky by the arm and led him out of the hall into the anteroom and, in the presence of a lackey, said coldly to him: "Several days ago Your Radiance was shown the door in a certain house. I shall not enter into explanations with you now, but I have the honour to inform you that if you come to my house again I shall fling you through the window. I don't like your handwriting." The Count bowed, set his teeth, shrank together, and disappeared.

Preparations began for removing to town, on the Arbát,[7] where our house was situated. Probably my father himself no longer cared to remain in the villa; but it was evident that he had succeeded in persuading my mother not to make a row. Everything was done quietly, without haste; my mother even sent her compliments to the old Princess and expressed her regret that, owing to ill-health, she would be unable to see her before her departure. I prowled about like a crazy person, and desired but one thing,—that everything might come to an end as speedily as possible. One thought never quitted my head: how could she, a young girl,—well, and a princess into the bargain,—bring herself to such a step, knowing that my father was not a free man while she had the possibility of marrying Byelovzóroff at least, for example? What had she hoped for? How was it that she had not been afraid to ruin her whole future?—"Yes,"— I thought,—"that's what love is,—that is passion,—that is devotion," ... and I recalled Lúshin's words to me: "Self-sacrifice is sweet—for some people." Once I happened to catch sight of a white spot in one of the windows of the wing.... "Can that be Zinaída's face?"—I thought; ... and it really was her face. I could not hold out. I could not part from her without bidding her a last farewell. I seized a convenient moment and betook myself to the wing.

In the drawing-room the old Princess received me with her customary, slovenly-careless greeting.

"What has made your folks uneasy so early, my dear fellow?"—she said, stuffing snuff up both her nostrils. I

---

[7] A square in Moscow.—Translator.

looked at her, and a weight was removed from my heart. The word "note of hand" uttered by Philípp tormented me. She suspected nothing ... so it seemed to me then, at least. Zinaída made her appearance from the adjoining room in a black gown, pale, with hair out of curl; she silently took me by the hand and led me away to her room.

"I heard your voice,"—she began,—"and came out at once. And did you find it so easy to desert us, naughty boy?"

"I have come to take leave of you, Princess,"—I replied,—"probably forever. You may have heard we are going away."

Zinaída gazed intently at me.

"Yes, I have heard. Thank you for coming. I was beginning to think that I should not see you.—Think kindly of me. I have sometimes tormented you; but nevertheless I am not the sort of person you think I am."

She turned away and leaned against the window-casing.

"Really, I am not that sort of person. I know that you have a bad opinion of me."

"I?"

"Yes, you ... you."

"I?"—I repeated sorrowfully, and my heart began to quiver as of old, beneath the influence of the irresistible, inexpressible witchery.—"I? Believe me, Zinaída Alexándrovna, whatever you may have done, however you may have tormented me, I shall love and adore you until the end of my life."

She turned swiftly toward me and opening her arms widely, she clasped my head, and kissed me heartily and warmly. God knows whom that long, farewell kiss was seeking, but I eagerly tasted its sweetness. I knew that it would never more be repeated.—"Farewell, farewell!" I kept saying....

She wrenched herself away and left the room. And I withdrew also. I am unable to describe the feeling with which I retired. I should not wish ever to have it repeated; but I should consider myself unhappy if I had never experienced it.

We removed to town. I did not speedily detach myself from the past, I did not speedily take up my work. My wound healed slowly; but I really had no evil feeling toward my father. On the contrary, he seemed to have gained in stature in my eyes ... let the psychologists explain this contradiction as best they may. One day I was walking along the boulevard when, to my indescribable joy, I encountered Lúshin. I liked him for his straightforward, sincere character; and, moreover, he was dear to me in virtue of the memories which he awakened in me. I rushed at him.

"Aha!"—he said, with a scowl.—"Is it you, young man? Come, let me have a look at you. You are still all sallow, and yet there is not the olden trash in your eyes. You look like a man, not like a lap-dog. That's good. Well, and how are you? Are you working?"

I heaved a sigh. I did not wish to lie, and I was ashamed to tell the truth.

"Well, never mind,"—went on Lúshin,—"don't be afraid. The principal thing is to live in normal fashion and not to yield to impulses. Otherwise, where's the good? No matter whither the wave bears one—'tis bad; let a man stand on a stone if need be, but on his own feet. Here I am croaking ...

but Byelovzóroff—have you heard about him?"

"What about him? No."

"He has disappeared without leaving a trace; they say he has gone to the Caucasus. A lesson to you, young man. And the whole thing arises from not knowing how to say good-bye,—to break bonds in time. You, now, seem to have jumped out successfully. Look out, don't fall in again. Farewell."

"I shall not fall in,"—I thought.... "I shall see her no more." But I was fated to see Zinaída once more.

## XXI

My father was in the habit of riding on horseback every day; he had a splendid red-roan English horse, with a long, slender neck and long legs, indefatigable and vicious. Its name was Electric. No one could ride it except my father. One day he came to me in a kindly frame of mind, which had not happened with him for a long time: he was preparing to ride, and had donned his spurs. I began to entreat him to take me with him.

"Let us, rather, play at leap-frog,"—replied my father,—"for thou wilt not be able to keep up with me on thy cob."

"Yes, I shall; I will put on spurs also."

"Well, come along."

We set out. I had a shaggy, black little horse, strong on its feet and fairly spirited; it had to gallop with all its might, it is true, when Electric was going at a full trot; but nevertheless I did not fall behind. I have never seen such a horseman as my father. His seat was so fine and so carelessly-adroit that the horse under him seemed to be conscious of it and to take pride in it. We rode the whole length of all the boulevards, reached the Maidens' Field,[8] leaped over several enclosures (at first I was afraid to leap, but my father despised timid people, and I ceased to be afraid), crossed the Moscow river twice;—and I was beginning to think that we were on our way homeward, the more so as my father remarked that my horse was tired, when suddenly he turned away from me in the direction of the Crimean Ford, and galloped along the shore.—I dashed after him. When he came on a level with a lofty pile of old beams which lay heaped together, he sprang nimbly from Electric, ordered me to alight and, handing me the bridle of his horse, told me to wait for him on that spot, near the beams; then he turned into a narrow alley and disappeared. I began to pace back and forth along the shore, leading the horses after me and scolding Electric, who as he walked kept incessantly twitching his head, shaking himself, snorting and neighing; when I stood still, he alternately pawed the earth with his hoof, and squealed and bit my cob on the neck; in a word, behaved like a spoiled darling, *pur sang.* My father did not return. A disagreeable humidity was wafted from the river; a fine rain set in and mottled the stupid, grey beams, around which I was hovering and of which I was so heartily tired, with tiny, dark spots. Anxiety took possession of me, but still my father did not come. A Finnish sentry, also all grey, with a huge, old-fashioned shako, in the form of a pot, on his head, and armed with a halberd (why should there be a sentry, I thought, on the

---

[8]A great plain situated on the outskirts of the town. So called because (says tradition) it was here that annually were assembled the young girls who were sent, in addition to the money tribute, to the Khan, during the Tatár period, in the thirteenth and fourteenth centuries.—Translator.

shores of the Moscow river?), approached me, and turning his elderly, wrinkled face to me, he said:

"What are you doing here with those horses, my little gentleman? Hand them over to me; I'll hold them."

I did not answer him; he asked me for some tobacco. In order to rid myself of him (moreover, I was tortured by impatience), I advanced a few paces in the direction in which my father had retreated; then I walked through the alley to the very end, turned a corner, and came to a standstill. On the street, forty paces distant from me, in front of the open window of a small wooden house, with his back to me, stood my father; he was leaning his breast on the window-sill, while in the house, half concealed by the curtain, sat a woman in a dark gown talking with my father: the woman was Zinaída.

I stood rooted to the spot in amazement. I must confess that I had in nowise expected this. My first impulse was to flee. "My father will glance round," I thought,—"and then I am lost.".... But a strange feeling—a feeling more powerful than curiosity, more powerful even than jealousy, more powerful than fear,—stopped me. I began to stare, I tried to hear. My father appeared to be insisting upon something. Zinaída would not consent. I seem to see her face now—sad, serious, beautiful, and with an indescribable imprint of adoration, grief, love, and a sort of despair. She uttered monosyllabic words, did not raise her eyes, and only smiled—submissively and obstinately. From that smile alone I recognised my former Zinaída. My father shrugged his shoulders, and set his hat straight on his head—which was always a sign of impatience with him.... Then the words became audible: "*Vous devez vous séparer de cette.*".... Zinaída drew herself up and stretched out her hand.... Suddenly, before my very eyes, an incredible thing came to pass:— all at once, my father raised the riding-whip, with which he had been lashing the dust from his coat-tails,—and the sound of a sharp blow on that arm, which was bare to the elbow, rang out. I could hardly keep from shrieking, but Zinaída started, gazed in silence at my father, and slowly raising her arm to her lips, kissed the mark which glowed scarlet upon it.

My father hurled his riding-whip from him, and running hastily up the steps of the porch, burst into the house.... Zinaída turned round, and stretching out her arms, and throwing back her head, she also quitted the window.

My heart swooning with terror, and with a sort of alarmed perplexity, I darted backward; and dashing through the alley, and almost letting go of Electric, I returned to the bank of the river.... I could understand nothing. I knew that my cold and self-contained father was sometimes seized by fits of wild fury; and yet I could not in the least comprehend what I had seen.... But I immediately felt that no matter how long I might live, it would be impossible for me ever to forget that movement, Zinaída's glance and smile; that her image, that new image which had suddenly been presented to me, had forever imprinted itself on my memory. I stared stupidly at the river and did not notice that my tears were flowing. "She is being beaten,"—I thought.... "She is being beaten ... beaten...."

"Come, what ails thee?—Give me my horse!"—rang out my father's voice behind me.

I mechanically gave him the bridle. He sprang upon Electric ... the half-frozen horse reared on his hind legs and leaped forward half a fathom ... but my father speedily got him under control; he dug his spurs into his flanks and beat him on the neck with his fist.... "Ekh, I have no whip,"—he muttered.

I remembered the recent swish through the air and the blow of that same whip, and shuddered.

"What hast thou done with it?"—I asked my father, after waiting a little.

My father did not answer me and galloped on. I dashed after him. I was determined to get a look at his face.

"Didst thou get bored in my absence?"—he said through his teeth.

"A little. But where didst thou drop thy whip?"—I asked him again.

My father shot a swift glance at me.—"I did not drop it,"—he said,—"I threw it away."—He reflected for a space and dropped his head ... and then, for the first and probably for the last time, I saw how much tenderness and compunction his stern features were capable of expressing.

He set off again at a gallop, and this time I could not keep up with him; I reached home a quarter of an hour after him.

"That's what love is,"—I said to myself again, as I sat at night before my writing-table, on which copy-books and text-books had already begun to make their appearance,—"that is what passion is!... How is it possible not to revolt, how is it possible to endure a blow from any one whomsoever... even from the hand that is most dear? But evidently it can be done if one is in love.... And I ... I imagined...."

The last month had aged me greatly, and my love, with all its agitations and sufferings, seemed to me like something very petty and childish and wretched in comparison with that other unknown something at which I could hardly even guess, and which frightened me like a strange, beautiful but menacing face that one strives, in vain, to get a good look at in the semi-darkness....

That night I had a strange and dreadful dream. I thought I was entering a low, dark room.... My father was standing there, riding-whip in hand, and stamping his feet; Zinaída was crouching in one corner and had a red mark, not on her arm, but on her forehead ... and behind the two rose up Byelovzóroff, all bathed in blood, with his pale lips open, and wrathfully menacing my father.

Two months later I entered the university, and six months afterward my father died (of an apoplectic stroke) in Petersburg, whither he had just removed with my mother and myself. A few days before his death my father had received a letter from Moscow which had agitated him extremely.... He went to beg something of my mother and, I was told, even wept,—he, my father! On the very morning of the day on which he had the stroke, he had begun a letter to me in the French language: "My son,"—he wrote to me,— "fear the love of women, fear that happiness, that poison...." After his death my mother sent a very considerable sum of money to Moscow.

## XXII

Four years passed. I had but just left the university, and did not yet quite know what to do with myself, at what door to knock; in the meanwhile, I was lounging about without occupation. One fine evening I encountered Maidánoff in the theatre. He had contrived to marry and enter the government service; but I found him unchanged. He went into unnecessary raptures, just as of old, and became low-spirited as suddenly as ever.

"You know,"—he said to me,—"by the way, that Madame Dólsky is here."

"What Madame Dólsky?"

"Is it possible that you have forgotten? The former Princess Zasyékin, with whom we were all in love, you included. At the villa, near Neskútchny Park, you remember?"

"Did she marry Dólsky?"

"Yes."

"And is she here in the theatre?"

"No, in Petersburg; she arrived here a few days ago; she is preparing to go abroad."

"What sort of a man is her husband?"—I asked.

"A very fine young fellow and wealthy. He's my comrade in the service, a Moscow man. You understand—after that scandal ... you must be well acquainted with all that ..." (Maidánoff smiled significantly), "it was not easy for her to find a husband; there were consequences ... but with her brains everything is possible. Go to her; she will be delighted to see you. She is handsomer than ever."

Maidánoff gave me Zinaída's address. She was stopping

in the Hotel Demuth. Old memories began to stir in me.... I promised myself that I would call upon my former "passion" the next day. But certain affairs turned up: a week elapsed, and when, at last, I betook myself to the Hotel Demuth and inquired for Madame Dólsky I learned that she had died four days previously, almost suddenly, in childbirth.

Something seemed to deal me a blow in the heart. The thought that I might have seen her but had not, and that I should never see her,—that bitter thought seized upon me with all the force of irresistible reproach. "Dead!" I repeated, staring dully at the door-porter, then quietly made my way to the street and walked away, without knowing whither. The whole past surged up at one blow and stood before me. And now this was the way it had ended, this was the goal of that young, fiery, brilliant life? I thought that—I pictured to myself those dear features, those eyes, those curls in the narrow box, in the damp, underground gloom,—right there, not far from me, who was still alive, and, perchance, only a few paces from my father.... I thought all that, I strained my imagination, and yet—

> From a mouth indifferent I heard the news of
> death,
> And with indifference did I receive it—

resounded through my soul. O youth, youth! Thou carest for nothing: thou possessest, as it were, all the treasures of the universe; even sorrow comforts thee, even melancholy becomes thee; thou are self-confident and audacious; thou sayest: "I alone live—behold!"—But the days speed on and vanish without a trace and without reckoning, and everything vanishes in thee, like wax in the sun, like snow.... And perchance the whole secret of thy charm consists not in the power to do everything, but in the possibility of thinking that thou wilt do everything—consists precisely in the fact that thou scatterest to the winds thy powers which thou hast not understood how to employ in any other way,—in the fact that each one of us seriously regards himself as a prodigal, seriously assumes that he has a right to say: "Oh, what could I not have done, had I not wasted my time!"

And I myself ... what did I hope for, what did I expect, what rich future did I foresee, when I barely accompanied with a single sigh, with a single mournful emotion, the spectre of my first love which had arisen for a brief moment?

And what has come to pass of all for which I hoped? Even now, when the shades of evening are beginning to close in upon my life, what is there that has remained for me fresher, more precious than the memory of that morning spring thunder-storm which sped so swiftly past?

But I calumniate myself without cause. Even then, at that frivolous, youthful epoch, I did not remain deaf to the sorrowful voice which responded within me to the triumphant sound which was wafted to me from beyond the grave. I remember that a few days after I learned of Zinaída's death I was present, by my own irresistible longing, at the death-bed of a poor old woman who lived in the same house with us. Covered with rags, with a sack under her head, she died heavily and with difficulty. Her whole life had been passed in a bitter struggle with daily want; she had seen no joy, she had not tasted the honey of happiness—it seemed as though she could not have failed to rejoice at death, at her release, her repose. But nevertheless, as long as her decrepit body held out, as long as her breast heaved under the icy hand which was laid upon it, until her last strength deserted her, the old woman kept crossing herself and whispering:—"O Lord, forgive my sins,"—and only with the last spark of consciousness did there vanish from her eyes the expression of fear and horror at her approaching end. And I remember that there, by the bedside of that poor old woman, I felt terrified for Zinaída, and felt like praying for her, for my father—and for myself.

# A NOTE ON LITERATURE

LITERATURE, like any other art, is singularly interesting to the artist; and, in a degree peculiar to itself among the arts, it is useful to mankind. These are the sufficient justifications for any young man or woman who adopts it as the business of his life. I shall not say much about the wages. A writer can live by his writing. If not so luxuriously as by other trades, then less luxuriously. The nature of the work he does all day will more affect his happiness than the quality of his dinner at night. Whatever be your calling, and however much it brings you in the year, you could still, you know, get more by cheating. We all suffer ourselves to be too much concerned about a little poverty; but such considerations should not move us in the choice of that which is to be the business and justification of so great a portion of our lives; and like the missionary, the patriot, or the philosopher, we should all choose that poor and brave career in which we can do the most and best for mankind. Now Nature, faithfully followed, proves herself a careful mother. A lad, for some liking to the jingle of words, betakes himself to letters for his life; by-and-by, when he learns more gravity, he finds that he has chosen better than he knew; that if he earns little, he is earning it amply; that if he receives a small wage, he is in a position to do considerable services; that it is in his power, in some small measure, to protect the oppressed and to defend the truth. So kindly is the world arranged, such great profit may arise from a small degree of human reliance on oneself, and such, in particular, is the happy star of this trade of writing, that it should combine pleasure and profit to both parties, and be at once agreeable, like fiddling, and useful, like good preaching.

GEOFFREY CHAUCER

BEN JONSON

SIR PHILLIP SIDNEY

EDMUND SPENSER

. . . . . . .

Man is imperfect; yet, in his literature, he must express himself and his own views and preferences; for to do anything else is to do a far more perilous thing than to risk being immoral: it is to be sure of being untrue. To ape a sentiment, even a good one, is to travesty a sentiment; that will not be helpful. To conceal a sentiment, if you are sure you hold it, is to take a liberty with truth. There is probably no point of view possible to a sane man but contains some truth and, in the true connection, might be profitable to the race. I am not afraid of the truth, if any one could tell it me, but I am afraid of parts of it impertinently uttered. There is a time to dance and a time to mourn; to be harsh as well as to be sentimental; to be ascetic as well as to glorify the appetites; and if a man were to combine all these extremes into his work, each in its place and proportion, that work would be the world's masterpiece of morality as well as of art. Partiality is immorality; for any book is wrong that gives a misleading picture of the world and life. The trouble is that the weakling must be partial; the work of one proving dank and depressing; of another, cheap and vulgar; of a third, epileptically sensual; of a fourth, sourly ascetic. In literature as in conduct, you can never hope to do exactly right. All you can do is to make as sure as possible; and for that there is but one rule. Nothing should be done in a hurry that can be done slowly. It is no use to write a book and put it by for nine or even ninety years; for in the writing you will have partly convinced yourself; the delay must precede any beginning; and if you meditate a work of art, you should first long roll the subject under the tongue to make sure you like the flavour, before you brew a volume that shall taste of it from end to end; or if you propose to enter on the field of controversy, you should first have thought upon the question under all conditions, in health as well as in sickness, in sorrow as well as in joy. It is this nearness of examination necessary for any true and kind writing, that makes the practice of the art a prolonged and noble education for the writer.

There is plenty to do, plenty to say, or to say over again, in the meantime. Any literary work which conveys faithful facts or pleasing impressions is a service to the public. It is even a service to be thankfully proud of having rendered. The slightest novels are a blessing to those in distress, not chloroform itself a greater. Our fine old sea-captain's life was justified when Carlyle soothed his mind with *The King's Own* or *Newton Forster*. To please is to serve; and so far from its being difficult to instruct while you amuse, it is difficult to do the one thoroughly without the other. Some part of the writer or his life will crop out in even a vapid book; and to read a novel that was conceived with any force is to multiply experience and to exercise the sympathies.

JOHN DRYDEN

FRANCIS BACON

Every article, every piece of verse, every essay, every *entre-filet*, is destined to pass, however swiftly, through the minds of some portion of the public, and to colour, however transiently, their thoughts. When any subject falls to be discussed, some scribbler on a paper has the invaluable opportunity of beginning its discussion in a dignified and human spirit; and if there were enough who did so in our public press, neither the public nor the Parliament would find it in their minds to drop to meaner thoughts. The writer has the chance to stumble, by the way, on something pleasing, something interesting, something encouraging, were it only to a single reader. He will be unfortunate, indeed, if he suit no one. He has the chance, besides, to stumble on something that a dull person shall be able to comprehend; and for a dull person to have read anything and, for that once, comprehended it, makes a marking epoch in his education.

JOSEPH ADDISON

JONATHAN SWIFT

Here, then, is work worth doing and worth trying to do well. And so, if I were minded to welcome any great accession to our trade, it should not be from any reason of a higher wage, but because it was a trade which was useful in a very great and in a very high degree; which every honest tradesman could make more serviceable to mankind in his single strength; which was difficult to do well and possible to do better every year; which called for scrupulous thought on the part of all who practised it, and hence became a perpetual education to their nobler natures; and which, pay it as you please, in the large majority of the best cases will still be underpaid. For surely, at this time of day in the nineteenth century, there is nothing that an honest man should fear more timorously than getting and spending more than he deserves.

ALEXANDER POPE

ROBERT BURNS

SAMUEL JOHNSON

OLIVER GOLDSMITH

•　　•　　•　　•　　•　　•　　•

The most influential books, and the truest in their influence, are works of fiction. They do not pin the reader to a dogma, which he must afterwards discover to be inexact; they do not teach him a lesson, which he must afterwards unlearn. They repeat, they rearrange, they clarify the lessons of life; they disengage us from ourselves, they constrain us to the acquaintance of others; and they show us the web of experience, not as we can see it for ourselves, but with a singular change—that monstrous, consuming *ego* of ours being, for the nonce, struck out. To be so, they must be reasonably true to the human comedy; and any work that is so serves the turn of instruction. But the course of our education is answered best by those poems and romances where we breathe a magnanimous atmosphere of thought and meet generous and pious characters.

WM. M. THACKERAY

GEORGE ELIOT

Excerpt from *Essays in the Art of Writing* by R. L. Stevenson.

Made in the USA
Las Vegas, NV
27 December 2022

64257491R00059